THE MISSING BUREAUCRAT

Other books by Hans Scherfig
in English from Fjord Press:

Stolen Spring (1986)
The Dead Man (Fall 1988)
Idealists (Spring 1989)
The Lost Monkey (Fall 1989)

Hans Scherfig

THE MISSING BUREAUCRAT

Translated from the Danish by Frank Hugus

*Fjord Press
Seattle
1988*

Translation copyright © 1988 Frank Hugus
All rights reserved. No part of this book may be reproduced
in any form, except for the purposes of a review, without the
written permission of the publisher.

Title of Danish edition: Den forsvundne fuldmægtig
Originally published in 1938 by Gyldendalske Boghandel,
Nordisk Forlag A/s, Copenhagen

Published and distributed by:
Fjord Press
P.O. Box 16501
Seattle, Washington 98116
(206) 625-9363

Editors: Steve Murray & Tiina Nunnally
Design & typography: Fjord Press Typography, Seattle
Cover design: Art Chantry Design, Seattle
Front cover illustration: Hans Scherfig, © 1938.
Back cover photograph: from *Hans Scherfig – Forfatteren,
    maleren, kommunisten* (Copenhagen: Forlaget Tiden, 1985)
Printed by Malloy Lithographing, Inc., Ann Arbor

Library of Congress Cataloging in Publication Data:

Scherfig, Hans, 1905–1979
  [Forsvundne fuldmægtig. English]
  The missing bureaucrat / Hans Scherfig ; translated from
the Danish by Frank Hugus. — 1st ed.
    p.   cm.
  Translation of: Den forsvundne fuldmægtig.
  Bibliography : p.
  ISBN 0-940242-26-5 (alk. paper) : $17.95.
ISBN 0-940242-25-7 (pbk. : alk. paper) : $8.95
  I. Title.
PT8175.S36F613   1988
839.8'1372—dc 19   88-10999 CIP

Printed in the United States of America
First edition, 1988

PART ONE

[1]

IN THE BEGINNING of October last year two men disappeared in Copenhagen. Their disappearances were reported to the police a few days apart. But otherwise the missing men apparently had nothing to do with each other.

One of the missing men was a recluse and eccentric who lived in the direst of economic straits. The other was the head of a family and a government official, sheltered and safeguarded in every respect. Their personalities and ways of life were probably as different as they could be.

That the police made a connection between the two cases at all was primarily because it was impossible to form an opinion about the reason for the disappearance of either individual. Another circumstance the police considered curious was the fact that the two missing men were the same age. They were born in the same year. This might appear to be a coincidence, but the fact that someone noticed this minor detail contributed to the solution of the case.

It was rather quickly established that at least one of the two men had committed suicide in a strange and ghastly manner. But it took some time for the police to figure out which one of them it was. Until a suicide note from the victim was discovered, it was impossible to establish the identity of the body found on Amager Common.

The fact that the police did not learn about the existence of this note until several days after the suicide had taken place was due solely to the methodical nature and the administrative sense of duty on the part of a certain Section Chief in the War Ministry. One cannot fault a government official for his methodical nature. But in this instance the work of the police and the solution of the case were delayed and made more difficult because of this unusual fact.

But even after the discovery of the above-mentioned suicide note, a great deal remained obscure and impenetrable. It took almost an entire year before the police would finally consider the case closed. They worked quietly with the very slim leads available. It was extremely conscientious and painstaking work, and no detail, no matter how small, was overlooked. Some seemingly totally insignificant reports that the police received from private citizens—namely from a barber in North Sjælland and from a former head teacher at Copenhagen's Metropolitan School—proved to be of critical importance.

It was one of the most difficult tasks the police had ever faced. When the facts finally became known, they not only created a sensation, they aroused widespread admiration. The newspapers were certainly correct when they wrote that it was the exemplary organization of the police force and the excellent cooperation among its various departments that deserved the credit for solving this strange case.

The establishment of the new National Police Force was certainly also of crucial significance in this case.

[2]

THE FIRST REPORT to the police came from a Mrs. Amsted.

She telephoned Police Headquarters at approximately 8 o'clock in the evening. Her husband, Head Clerk Teodor Amsted, hadn't come home from the office yet. He always came home at precisely twenty minutes past five every day. He was a very punctual man. He left his office in the red-brick Ministry building at 5 o'clock. And it took him exactly twenty minutes to walk home to his apartment in the Gammelholm district. He took the shortest route and maintained a steady, even pace.

He was very careful to step in the center of the flagstones and avoid the cracks in between. It was also important for him to make sure to step on certain manhole covers located along his route. And if, on rare occasions, he happened to be walking along lost in thought and forgot this duty, he might just turn around and walk back and tread firmly on a particular cover. He was a man with a strong sense of duty and felt out of sorts if he neglected to do something he was supposed to do.

Only if the weather was very bad would he take the streetcar. But that made no difference in the time it took him to get home. The streetcar lines were inconveniently located. He could ride for only two stops. He would get off at the statue of Niels Juel and would still have to walk the length of Niels Juelsgade and a little way down Herluf Trollesgade.

Mrs. Amsted had phoned his office, of course, and a secretary who was working late was able to tell her that Head Clerk Amsted had already left at about 2 o'clock. He had received a letter which seemed to have made quite an impression on him. He had been very nervous and had forgotten his brown briefcase and his walking stick when he left.

This information made Mrs. Amsted quite anxious. As the hours slowly passed, she finally saw no alternative but to call the police.

Even if something out of the ordinary had happened, her husband certainly could have called home. He had never kept any secrets from her. Theirs was an absolutely happy marriage. It was totally out of the question for one of them to go out alone. During the eighteen years they had been married, they had always been together. She simply couldn't imagine who could have written to her husband, or why the letter had been sent to the Ministry instead of to their address on Herluf Trollesgade.

That he might know some other woman with whom he corresponded without his wife's knowledge was absolutely unthinkable.

She knew everything about her husband. There was nothing in his life or in his soul or on his body that she didn't have complete knowledge of and control over.

"Well now, let's just wait and see," the policeman said. "If he'd been run over or been injured in some way, we'd have been notified by the fire department or the rescue squad. No injured party by the name of Teodor Amsted has been taken to any hospital in the city or its environs. Or anybody whose name the police don't know."

This did not reassure Mrs. Amsted at all. Not once in eighteen years had her husband come home later than twenty minutes past five. Only once had he left his office early. That was the time he had an abscessed tooth, and the pain had suddenly become so intense that he couldn't stand it. But of course then he had called home before he went to the dentist.

The letter addressed to him at the Ministry was simply incomprehensible. Who in the world would write to him?

Mrs. Amsted knew that as a sixteen-year-old high school boy her husband had had a highly platonic crush on a lady in a newspaper kiosk. She even knew about the poem that the young Amsted had written to the lady:

> *Thus you sit in narrow kiosk caged,*
> *Spring-sweetly smiling behind your narrow window,*
> *While I outside must stand as rain and wind do blow.*

But she had long since forgiven him this trifling juvenile aberration. Whenever she mentioned it to him, it was only in a playful and teasing way which made him blush and laugh.

No. He had no secrets from his wife. The whole thing was incomprehensible and insane.

Mrs. Amsted had wept. "What could have happened to Papa? What could have happened?" she repeated incessantly.

And their boy, thirteen-year-old Leif, cried too, his teeth chattering as if he were freezing. He was a pale, thin boy with completely white hair.

Supper got cold and was warmed up again several times. It was fish balls in celery sauce. Celery sauce was just about the worst thing Leif could imagine. In the midst of his tears he felt a certain glee that the eating of the hated fish balls and celery had been postponed.

On the whole there was something strangely pleasurable and titillating about the situation — something out of the ordinary, something sensational in an otherwise painfully regimented and orderly life.

When the food was finally put on the table, his mother didn't have the strength to force him to clean his plate. Usually she always said, "You'll never be big and strong if you don't clean your plate! Celery and fish balls are the healthiest things there are. Take my word for it, Leif the Lucky ate *his* fish balls in celery sauce!"

Leif the Lucky — that renowned Viking and seafarer — was always held up as an example when he couldn't clean his plate or do his math homework.

Mrs. Amsted cleared the table without noticing the leftover pieces of celery at the edge of Leif's plate. Usually these last cold mouthfuls were precisely the ones it was so important to force down the boy's throat. Once when he was younger, he had stored a mouthful of food for an entire evening. It was impossible for him to swallow it. He hid it in one of his cheeks for several hours, baffling his parents by his silence. But it was discovered when he tried to spit the gooey wad into his handkerchief. Then there was an awful fuss. Both Leif the Lucky and the numerous poor children who would be happy to have his good food were held up as examples. Why, someday he would starve if he continued to act that way! Leif thought that sounded marvelous. He didn't like food.

Tonight his homework was forgotten too. His mother usually checked him on his history and geography. Father had to take care of math and German.

The battles that were waged every evening in the home on Herluf Trollesgade were exhausting. But then Leif was one of the best students in his class. Even though it cost him tears. His father had been among the best students in his class too. And that had also cost tears. It was in the same old gray school on Frue Plads which *his* father before him had attended as well. There were traditions in the Amsted family.

Mrs. Amsted kept going over to the window and looking out into the dark, empty Herluf Trollesgade. But she was careful to walk around the spot where the carpet always showed so much wear.

It was raining. The wind was blowing so hard that the thermometer outside the window rattled. You could hear the streetcars up at Kongens Nytorv. Down at the harbor the steamships were blowing their whistles.

The apartment still smelled of celery. The patterned linoleum in the dining room also had its own odor. But linoleum was so easy to *keep clean*, Mrs. Amsted liked to say.

The large clock on the sideboard ticked loudly. And every time the clock struck, Mrs. Amsted would give a start in fright. "Nine! And he's still not home.—Nine thirty!—Ten o'clock! Still not..."

[3]

THE POLICE DIDN'T GET the second report of a disappearance until several days later.

A lady in Rosengade—a Mrs. Møller—reported that her lodger, Mikael Mogensen, who lived in a garret above her apartment, had not been home for three days and three nights. She therefore assumed that he must have been involved in an accident.

He owed her the previous month's rent, 15 kroner, and if he had cleared out, she would have to ask the police to find him or permit her to recoup her loss by, if necessary, selling what he had left behind.

Fifteen kroner was actually no small amount for the garret she had rented out to Mikael Mogensen. It had no real door, only a lathwork grill, so that you could look in at him from the hall. And the room was unfurnished. Mogensen slept on the floor on several layers of old newspapers with an old black briefcase beneath his head. There was a big stack of books in one corner. In another corner a pile of newspapers. In a third corner was the "kitchen," that is, a hazardous primus stove, a frying pan, a casserole dish, and alcohol and kerosene.

Mogensen was a bohemian who was well-known in that neighborhood, especially to the children. He had long, untrimmed hair and a full beard. He always walked around in an extremely old, tattered overcoat with his old black briefcase under his arm. No one had any idea what he had in the briefcase, and people came up with the strangest notions.

"But he was a gentle, quiet person," Mrs. Møller said. "Why, he wouldn't even harm a cat." She said she thought he came from a good family and had been a student at the university at one time. But something seemed to have snapped inside, so he was never able to make it. He wasn't a drunk. He didn't run around with women either. He wasn't the least bit dissipated. On the contrary, he was a pure ascetic.

He was always reading thick books. Foreign ones too, which Mrs. Møller wasn't able to read. And he spoke a refined and cultivated Danish. He certainly could have gone far; if he had wanted to, that is. But something must have happened to him once, since he had turned out to be so strange.

He was well liked by the other people who lived on Rosengade. He always tipped his hat politely whenever he met anyone. This short little street was like a little provincial town where they all knew each other. It was a small, closed society. The residents kept to their own street, only rarely and reluctantly venturing to other parts of the city.

By and large they were lower-middle-class people who had had a run of bad luck. People whose lives had gone to pieces. Shipwrecked people who had been stranded on this street. It was the island of dead ships.

But ugly and horrible things also took place on Rosengade. Even though it was small and short, there were plenty of tenements in back, around the dark courtyards.

There were four or five dives where people could drink port after closing time. There was a brothel where the couples lay in bunk beds. There was a "wise woman" who performed gruesome, illegal operations. And there was the lady in the black rain cape. The one who lived alone with a large dog.

There were several prostitutes of varying ages. The blonde lady in the ice cream store was close to sixty. She dated back to the old days before public prostitution had been outlawed. Little Maja was only nine years old. But she earned more than the fat blonde lady. Everybody on the street said she was a nice, well-brought-up little girl. She curtsied politely and held the door open for people going in or out. She had extraordinary shining eyes. And sometimes she had epileptic fits.

Mogensen greeted everyone politely. He minded his own business and never got involved in anything that was happening on the street. He was a gentleman. He strode with dignity along the street, wearing his old tattered coat and his boots with holes in them, with his mysterious briefcase under his arm. And he would ceremoniously tip his old greasy cap in greeting. Slightly stooped, slightly nearsighted, and very grimy, but full of serenity and dignity.

He spoke in a singular manner, using words that Mrs. Møller and the other people on the street didn't really understand. But there was certainly nothing evil about him.

That was why Mrs. Møller felt that Mogensen couldn't have done anything illegal that would have forced him to go into hiding. And as far as the 15 kroner he owed her for the rent was concerned, certainly that couldn't be the reason for his disappearance either. He had owed her money before, sometimes for as long as two months. It wasn't for the sake of the money that Mrs. Møller reported his disappearance to the police. She wasn't like that. She wasn't a monster. Things had to be done properly, of course, and she had to live too. And 15 kroner is a lot of money.

But she had told Mogensen, "I know you're a decent sort, Mogensen. You won't cheat me. I'm not worried about my 15 kroner."

And Mogensen had replied that there was indeed no reason to be worried. "This amount will be remitted to you in the course of next week, Mrs. Møller."

The only reason there had been a slight argument later was because it turned out that Mogensen had a lot of money on him. That was why Mrs. Møller felt that the conditions for the loan, so to speak, no longer applied. Especially since Mogensen was spending the money in an unreasonable and senseless way.

When a person can literally throw away more than a hundred kroner in a single evening, there's no excuse for him to owe rent money. Mrs. Møller had pointed that out to him, and he had taken offense.

"It is extraordinarily regrettable," he had said, "that one obviously can no longer depend on an agreement, Mrs. Møller. I expressly said *next week*. And that is what you consented to. In the meantime I intend to use the money for purposes which I myself find appropriate."

And when she repeated her criticism concerning the large amount of money that had been squandered in such a senseless fashion, he had used harsh and abusive language. "You are a lowly person, Mrs. Møller! A man such as myself cannot allow himself to enter into an altercation with you. I sincerely despise you."

A lot of bystanders outside had overheard this and had laughed about it. Mrs. Olsen from the basement ice cream store had even shouted, "That's right, Mogensen! Ignore her!" And this had all taken place in Mrs. Møller's own living room. Those were the last words she ever heard from Mikael Mogensen.

The next day he had disappeared. The strange party that had cost so much money had been a kind of farewell party.

[4]

On October 10th, the day after Mrs. Amsted reported her husband's disappearance, an appalling discovery was made on Amager Common.

A soldier, who had been participating in the army's live ammunition exercises, found the horribly mutilated remains of a human being who had quite literally been blasted to smithereens.

The soldier had been sent out with a couple of other men to look for an artillery shell which hadn't exploded on impact and would be extremely dangerous if it were found by children or some other unsuspecting person.

Not far from the spot where the embankment above Kalvebod Strand joins the island of Amager, he discovered a large hole in the ground similar to one left by an explosion. To his horror he found bits of clothing and the bloody remains of a human being literally splattered all over the place.

The police were notified immediately. Together with the army's demolition experts they set an extensive investigation in motion.

The explosion must have been unusually powerful. It probably hadn't been seen or heard by anyone because at that very moment the army was conducting heavy artillery exercises using live ammunition. The roar of the detonation had no doubt been mistaken for cannon fire; people must have assumed that the explosion was an artillery shell landing.

The sight that confronted the police was so appalling that even the afternoon newspapers were forced to refrain from giving a detailed account of it.

The experts established that the victim must have put dynamite everywhere on his body. His pockets, hat, shoes, etc. had contained explosives. In fact, he even must have put dynamite in his mouth.

Identifying the body was out of the question under these circumstances. Several extremely small bits of gray clothing were sent off for a thorough chemical examination, and the remains of a pocket watch were closely studied.

Strangely enough this watch hadn't been completely pulverized, but merely damaged, the way it would have been if someone had flung it against a rock or stomped on it. It was found several meters away from the hole the explosion had made in the ground.

It had even been possible to find a fingerprint on the back of the watch. And it was also established beyond all doubt that the watch had stopped at 2:34. But naturally these things could shed no light on the identity of the victim.

The police went about their task with commendable thoroughness. They dug up and sifted all the ground around the scene of the disaster. They made plaster of Paris impressions of footprints. They dusted the area and took pictures. They meticulously collected tiny little things such as pieces of buttons, coins, bits of leather, etc. and subjected them to a systematic examination. They called into play all the methods of modern technology.

It took the better part of a week before the results of these investigations were made public. Concerning the bits of clothing that had been found, the police ascertained that they consisted of a gray, pure wool, double-woven worsted cloth of English fabrication. Part of a trademark in the lining could in fact be reconstructed as a "C.D.," which they interpreted as "Chestertown-Deverill," the well-known English fabric manufacturer.

As luck would have it, only one master tailor in Copenhagen had the exclusive rights to this high-quality material. And the police went to work examining his customer files.

Among the master tailor's regular customers was the missing bureaucrat, Teodor Amsted.

But even before the police could make their inquiries at the missing bureaucrat's home, and before they could make comparisons of the fingerprint on the watch with any possible fingerprints in Mr. Amsted's residence or office, the police learned about a letter from the missing man. A letter that had been received in Section 14 of the War Ministry.

This letter was a suicide note in which Teodor Amsted revealed his unhappy decision.

In a way everything seemed obvious. But it turned out later that there was still a great deal of mystery surrounding the suicide of the unfortunate head clerk.

[5]

WHEN THE MIDDAY NEWSPAPER was delivered to Section 14 of the War Ministry at 11:00, it was first opened and read (without any protest from the others in the office) by young Deputy Clerk Hougaard, whose father was a former Secretary of the Royal Privy Council.

When he had finished reading he passed the newspaper along to Miss Lilienfeldt; her father being a colonel, she was accordingly next in line after Mr. Hougaard. In this way the newspaper made its rounds and was read by everyone in the office in a sequential order corresponding to each individual's origin and rank.

The mail that arrived in Section 14 of the War Ministry was handled in accordance with immutable rules established by long routine. Letters of every conceivable class and category arrived. The letters were opened, sorted, recorded, initialed, stamped, and read according to an exacting system and in a strictly prescribed sequence.

Some letters concerned national defense. Some letters were of vital importance for national security. And some letters were of secondary importance. Such as a bill from a glazier regarding a newly installed windowpane: due to a lack of circumspection on the part of the office personnel in the positioning of a window latch, an accident occurred entailing the fracturing of one of the Ministry's windowpanes, the wind having induced the aforesaid window to slam.

There were letters, applications, suggestions, and projects that were supposed to be routed to the Department Head or to the Defense Minister. There were letters that were supposed to be answered by the Section Chief. There were letters that weren't supposed to be answered at all, but returned after they were provided with an appropriate marginal notation and after their serial number and file designation had been recorded.

The Ministry had its own special alphabet—a system of specific marks and hieroglyphics—which the Section Chief inscribed on the correspondence in red or blue pencil and which indicated to the initiated what further action was to be accorded to the document in question.

It is understandable then that a letter addressed to Section 14 of the War Ministry must of necessity lie dormant for a period of time and go through a certain set procedure before it can be read, and before it can be answered.

The morning after Head Clerk Amsted disappeared, a letter arrived at the office in the mail, addressed to the Section Chief personally. This circumstance resulted in its reaching him significantly faster than other letters that had arrived at the same time. But because of the peculiar and rigid system of mail sorting, the better part of a week would inevitably pass before it was read by the Section Chief.

It was obvious that the contents of the letter made an unusual impression on him. His voice was completely hoarse when he called Head Clerk Degerstrøm into his private office and told him to be seated.

"Something has happened. Something unprecedented and unseemly. Something that concerns the honor of the office—in fact, of the Ministry itself."

Head Clerk Degerstrøm listened attentively.

"I consider it my duty to inform you of it. All the more so since I am convinced it cannot in the long run remain unknown to the public at large. Head Clerk Amsted is dead."

"He's dead?" Head Clerk Degerstrøm's first thought inevitably had to be that he would therefore be next in line for advancement when the Section Chief some day reached an appropriate age. In this office everybody waited patiently for time to pass. Only with the aid of time could a person advance to a higher rank.

"He died in a disgraceful manner. He took his own life. I'm sitting here with a letter which he addressed to me personally and in which he considered it of vital urgency to communicate his motives for the step he has undertaken.

"First of all he states that under these circumstances we cannot expect to see him at the office again. The key to his cabinet and desk drawer is to be found at his home on Herluf Trollesgade. The reason he found it imperative to communicate his suicide to us is because of the unusual method he employed, inasmuch as he assumed it would not leave any possibility of identifying his remains: he has blown himself up by filling not only his pockets with dynamite but also his hat and his mouth."

"So he was the one — the one on Amager Common."

"Yes, he was the one. He was the one the newspapers wrote all those things about. And now the office will also be mentioned in connection with this scandal."

"Oh my God!"

"Yes. You can say that again."

"This is terrible!"

"Yes."

"His poor family!"

"Yes."

"It's dreadful!"

"Yes. Now listen, there's more. He enjoins me to communicate what happened in as delicate a manner as possible to his wife. Concerning the motive for his action, he is only in a position to reveal that it was not due to his marital relationship or to any sort of erotic circumstance whatsoever. It was a purely personal dissatisfaction with his activities and achievements which prompted him to—"

"His activities? His activities here at the office? But how is it possible that they could have been dissatisfying?"

"Yes, that is highly incomprehensible. One did not have the impression that he was in any way unsuited for or discontent with his work here. But he does write in this (if you'll pardon the expression) 'farewell letter' that his expectations of life were unfulfilled."

"It seems quite incomprehensible."

"Yes, it does."

"Maybe he suddenly went insane."

"Yes, there is ample reason to assume that Head Clerk Amsted undertook his desperate act in a fit of insanity."

"Yes, of course. It's the only explanation. He was sick."

"Still, it's an awkward form of insanity. An extremely awkward form . . . It will now be my regrettable duty to report the receipt of this document to the criminal investigation department of the police force. I consider it necessary to do so by telephone. Whatever is to be undertaken subsequently must be a matter for the police to decide. Unfortunately one does not dare hope that the press will show the desirable discretion. We have to fear that this office will be mentioned in connection with this awkward and regrettable affair. I consider it my duty to prepare you for this."

"It is quite regrettable."

"Yes, exceedingly regrettable."

Head Clerk Degerstrøm made a motion to withdraw so that he could let the Section Chief's sensational piece of information circulate to the rest of the office staff. But the Section Chief stopped him.

"There is one more thing I wish to bring to the attention of the office staff. Under the existing circumstances, of course, there can be no question of official participation on the part of the office in connection with Head Clerk Amsted's funeral. If anyone employed here wishes to exhibit any form of sympathy or condolence to his surviving family in the form of wreaths, flowers, or the like, it must be done on a purely private basis.

The office as such is in no position to show such sympathy, and any official collection et cetera must not take place here."

[6]

A MAN IS RINGING the bell at Mrs. Amsted's front door. A man wearing a windbreaker and bicycle clips on his pants. He is easily recognizable as a detective.

"Please excuse me, Mrs. Amsted. Unfortunately I have to ask you a few questions in connection with what has happened."

"Yes, of course... come inside. But you understand... I'm so upset. It's more than a person can endure, what has happened to us. And now the police are here too!"

"I realize of course how painful it is for you. But I'll make this as brief as possible."

They went inside, down the very long, dark hallway.

"Please, have a seat. Please excuse how things look. Nothing has been tidied up here today. I gave the maid the day off. Everything has slipped out of its usual routine. So much has happened, you know. If I had known you were coming... You really must promise me that you won't look at anything in this mess..."

"Don't let it worry you. I'll avoid looking at anything, I assure you," said the detective, peering around the living room, where the most meticulous order prevailed.

The furniture was old-fashioned, heirlooms from Teodor Amsted's childhood home. Things that had surrounded him for the 46 years he had been alive.

The small mahogany bureau. The card table with its shiny double leaves that were turned up so that the Saxon porcelain would be reflected twofold. The oval table with its doily and crystal bowl in the middle and small books of poetry in leather bindings. The piano cover was up, in the Danish fashion, with music books open as if someone had just been playing.

"Oh, it's horrifying, horrifying. How could it ever have happened! I simply don't understand a thing. It's as if I'm dreaming and will soon wake up from this horror. We were so happy. I assure you we were. We were so completely and utterly happy. In the eighteen years we were married we were never apart for a single day. He would never think of going anywhere without taking me along... That's what makes it all so incomprehensible. He must have been sick. It clearly must have happened in some sudden attack of insanity! Don't you think so? Isn't that what the police think too?"

"Oh yes, yes. Of course. Did you notice anything unusual about your husband? Was he nervous?"

"No, no. Not at all. He was always so calm and even-tempered. We lived quite a normal life, you know. I always saw to it that things were orderly and pleasant for him."

"And there hasn't been anything peculiar or different about your husband recently?"

"No. How could you think such a thing! You should have known him. He was always the same. He was such a regular and methodical person. You might even say he was a creature of habit. He didn't like changes. Everything was supposed to be where it always had been. That's the way I am too. We always agreed on things.

"Oh, he was so kind, our little Papa. He was always so considerate of me. Oh, how could he do it! Oh, how could he put me in this situation! Oh, what will our friends say! And all the other people! The newspapers have written about it too. I hardly dare open a newspaper anymore."

Mrs. Amsted put her hands over her eyes and cried. The detective waited tactfully for her tears to subside.

"It's so incomprehensible, so insane. Oh, if I only knew *why*! And then to do it like *that*..."

"Yes, it's quite extraordinary. And that's exactly why I'm here. The police don't really understand it. There's so much that has to be looked into. In reality we have very little to go on, you see. You say you recognize what's left of his watch? The suit the deceased was wearing came from Master Tailor Holm's shop, where your husband had his suits made. And finally there's the letter. You're absolutely certain that he wrote it himself? That it's his handwriting?"

"Yes, I am. It's his letter. And his handwriting. His neat, methodical handwriting. Who else would have written it? Do you think it could have been somebody else? Do the police think maybe it wasn't him at all who... who died in that awful way?"

"Unfortunately there isn't any doubt. You should know his handwriting, after all. And of course we can compare it with other letters. Besides, who would be interested in writing a phony letter? It's just so strange that he didn't give any real reason. It's impossible to see any motive for his action."

"Yes, but do you think there can be any doubt? You must understand: I've made all the arrangements already. I've placed a notice in the newspaper—quite short and simple, the way he would have liked it. And of course there have been so many other things to take care of too. I have to think of mourning, after all—mourning apparel, I mean. You know how much there is to do when somebody dies. It was the same way when my father-in-law died..."

Through the French door the detective could see into the dining room. It was very long and not quite rectangular. The window was located in one corner, and very little light came in from the courtyard. It had dark paneling and an oak sideboard. A sewing machine stood on the dining room table. Some black material was spread out on it. Several dresses hung over the straightback chairs.

Mrs. Amsted followed his eyes. "Oh, you'll have to pardon all the mess. I was just sitting there sewing when you rang the doorbell. I've ripped the trim off a few dresses. I'm sending them out to be dyed. I'm expecting the delivery boy any minute. I thought it was him ringing the doorbell. They're to be dyed black. But tell me, do you think there can be the slightest doubt that it was my husband who . . . that he's the one who died?"

She clutched the detective's arm.

"You must tell me! You have to tell me the truth! Is it conceivable that he isn't really dead? That he might be wandering around and has lost his memory? Or could something else have happened? Was it somebody else entirely who was killed out on Amager Common? Or is it conceivable that he didn't kill himself? That somebody else . . . That he's been *murdered*?"

[7]

THE DETECTIVE TRIED GENTLY to free himself from her grasp.

"No, no, Mrs. Amsted. That isn't what I think at all. I just think that there's so much that can't be accounted for. We can't find any motive or any explanation. That's why you have to tell me everything. You mustn't hide anything from me. You must be calm and have faith in us. What you tell the police won't go any farther."

"Yes, but what do you want me to tell you?"

"Please don't get angry with me for being so blunt. Please answer me with complete candor. Are you absolutely certain that your husband didn't have any . . . acquaintanceship outside the home? Have you ever had any suspicions?"

Mrs. Amsted glared at him. "Must I really put up with this

sort of question? Must I really tolerate it? Here in my home! In *his* home!"

"Please don't take it that way, Mrs. Amsted. I have to ask you. I have to know everything. It's in everybody's interest that everything come to light. And of course there was that letter to the Ministry. The one which arrived just before your husband left the office and which apparently got him pretty worked up."

"I can only tell you that for my husband no one else existed but me. Leif and me. His *home*. It was his whole life!"

"And you have no idea who might have written that letter to the office?"

"No. None whatsoever. It's completely incomprehensible. He never kept anything secret from me. Nothing could ever happen that he wouldn't tell me about."

"But it does seem fairly certain that there was some sort of connection between the mysterious letter and your husband's desperate act. It would be of crucial importance if we could find out something about the contents of the letter or about who wrote it. Don't you have any idea at all? Can't you come up with something?"

"No. I can't think of a thing. I'm at a total loss. I've thought about that letter over and over. It has tormented me day and night. I can't imagine who wrote it. I just can't."

"How was your husband situated financially? Was he having difficulties of any kind?"

"My husband was not one of those people who goes into debt. His affairs were in order."

"Did your husband have life insurance?"

"Yes. Why do you ask? Yes, he did have life insurance. Fortunately he thought of making us secure while there was still time. He was so orderly with everything. Naturally I was afraid that the insurance wouldn't be paid now — now, under the present . . . circumstances. I read through the provisions. It's so complicated. But our lawyer says that it's all in order. He's such a marvelous person. He went to the university with my husband. Attorney Lund-Jensen. Perhaps you know him?"

"No. Do you have the life insurance policy here?"

"Yes. It's in the crystal bowl. Here it is. Please, if you want to take a look at it."

The policeman glanced through the papers.

"Yes indeed, it seems to be all in order. It's quite a large sum your husband was insured for. But it's been a long time since it was taken out. So I'm sure there won't be any objections to it."

"Yes, it was taken out right after we were married. We've always liked to have that sort of thing in order. In case anything happened to either of us. And now you can see that it was a good thing that we thought of the future. Since we've been making payments on it all these years, it would have been the last straw if it were invalidated when there was finally a need for it."

"When did you and your husband get married?"

"Eighteen years ago. It was the year he got his position — after his graduation."

"You have children? How many?"

"We have only Leif. Poor little Leif! I've sent him to my sister's — Head Surgeon Mörtel's wife — for these few days. This house is certainly no place for him while all of this is going on. He might hear something. Of course he knows that our little Papa is dead. But he mustn't know how it happened... But in the long run! How can he avoid finding out about it in the long run? Oh, how can a person bring so much sorrow to the ones he loves?"

"Are your husband's parents still living?"

"No, they're dead."

"Did your husband have any brothers or sisters?"

"No, he was an only child. Just like Leif."

"Do you know whether there was any mental illness in your husband's family?"

[8]

Mrs. Amsted had leaned back in her chair. She held her hands in front of her face as if she were thinking intently. Then she shook her head.

"Mental illness in his family? No, no! How can you possibly think that? In the *Amsted* family! How can you possibly ask me a question like that?"

"Mental illness can occur in the best of families, you know."

"Yes, well, there is absolutely nothing like that in my husband's family. Absolutely not! His father was such a fine old gentleman. Very distinguished and lovable. He was in the Ministry too, just like my husband. He was a section chief. And his mother was such a capable person. She ran the household by herself—sacrificed herself completely for her home. And she idolized her son. No... no... I never heard about anyone... anyone abnormal in his family. My husband's uncle was Supreme Court Magistrate Amsted. Another uncle was a provincial archdeacon. There was also a Department Head Amsted. He was a cousin of my husband's father. And the elder Mrs. Amsted's brother was *General Masen*. They were all very capable people in that family."

"Was there anything your husband was especially preoccupied with recently?"

"No. He was preoccupied with his work in the Ministry, of course. He was extremely conscientious and meticulous. He would often work on Ministry affairs here at home too. Of course I don't know anything about things like that. But I know he loved his work and was *devoted* to it. I never heard him say that he was dissatisfied or unhappy about anything at the Ministry. That's why what he wrote in his letter about his 'activities' being unsatisfying is so completely incomprehensible. I never heard him say that he had any desire to do anything else. Everyone in his family has been a government official, after all. Quite young, as a child, I think he wanted to be a poet or a scientist or something like that. But I never heard him complain about the calling that he chose in life and that he was literally born into... And he was so well liked by all his colleagues. Well liked and respected! We got together socially with most of them... But it was his *home* he was most fond of. He *loved* to be at home. He helped Leif with his homework, especially with his mathematics and German. Leif is our only child, you know. We *do* want him to make his way in life. Leif sometimes has trouble learning. It's as if his thoughts are someplace else. As if he had too much *imagination*. But I'm sure he'll grow out of it. That's what the principal thinks too. 'Quite a number of children have imaginations that are a little too vivid, but it passes — they grow out of it,' he says. But sometimes it certainly made my husband a little nervous. There's so much they have to know in school these days. Much more than when the rest of us were children. And of course you have to be at the top of the class if you want to get ahead in the world. And you have obligations when your father and grandfather were such capable men. That's what we've always told Leif too. 'Leif, being an Amsted has its obligations!' Especially on Thursdays, when Leif had his math assignments. Then we would all sit slaving away on them in the dining room. And Leif would cry. And I would be on the verge of tears too. And my husband would speak to him angrily. And it would get to be so late before we would finish. We've always said to Leif: '*Why* do you always wait until the last minute? You have the whole week to do it, but it *has* to wait until Thursday!'... But naturally these are just little things. He's actually doing quite well in school. Last year he was number four in his class. That's really quite good, isn't it?"

"Uh, oh, yes, it is."

"The principal told my husband a while ago, 'Leif is a *nice* boy!' We're proud of that."

"Did your husband have any special interests—aside from his work at the Ministry?"

"No, his *home* was everything to him. Well, actually there was his stamp collection too. He had over 6000 stamps—different ones, that is. He traded them with his colleagues in the Ministry. He subscribed to a philatelic magazine too and corresponded with collectors in both Switzerland and Holland. He was very involved in it. They weren't just ordinary stamps he would mount in albums. He was especially interested in blocks of four. You know, when four stamps are attached. And in printing errors and watermarks and that kind of thing. He would sit in there at his desk and work with his watermark detectors and tongs and perforation gauges and whatever all those things are called. He spent quite a bit of money on it too. But since he was interested in it, why not? Of course I don't really understand it. That's something for men. But actually I was glad he had that hobby. Other husbands so often have interests outside the home. Isn't that right? I was glad he had an interest that *tied* him to his home."

"Of course. Was there anything else that interested him or occupied his time?"

"No... well, yes. He did read a lot. Primarily the newspapers of course. And then the books that a person has to be familiar with. The latest things that come out, you know. And then sometimes he read some big volumes from the library too. But I think they were things for his work in the Ministry. In any event they were books about military matters and Napoleon and techniques of war and that sort of thing. Some of those books are still in there on his desk, in fact. I completely forgot to have them returned. So much has happened. I'm afraid they're overdue. But of course that's my fault. Teodor was always so particular about that kind of thing."

"Yes, yes. I'll have to take a look at your husband's papers. I'm sure you understand. Nothing will be disturbed. You can set your mind at ease. We will maintain the utmost discretion about everything we see, of course. But under the present circumstances we do have to try to find something that can give us a clue — just a slight hint of an explanation for what happened."

"Certainly. His study is in here." Mrs. Amsted opened the door. "Of course I can't tell the police not to do something. But you really could do just as well by asking me what you want to know. My husband had no secrets from me. Absolutely none. There is nothing in his possession that I don't know about. He never received a letter that he didn't show me. Nothing happened in his life that he didn't tell me about. Our married life wasn't like other people's. You mustn't think that. We meant *everything* to each other. Everything!"

The detective had walked into the study and was making a quick inspection of it. Mrs. Amsted blew a few puffs of air at a couple of specks of dust on the desk.

"You must forgive me that the stove isn't lit in here. And things haven't been straightened up in here today either. If I had only known you were coming! Normally we always have the whole apartment in order by 11 o'clock every day. But everything is so out of joint now. I'm terribly sorry that you have to see it like this. What must the police think! I'm really sorry that I gave the maid the day off."

"Please don't give it a thought, Mrs. Amsted. Things look lovely in here. And it wouldn't really matter anyway... Has anyone touched your husband's desk since his death?"

"No. Everything is just as he left it. I haven't even thought of tidying up yet. Oh, it gives me an eerie feeling to have to handle his things now. I've left everything just the way it was."

"Well, that's just fine."

The detective stood fingering several thick bound volumes

that were lying on the desk. He read the titles and nodded significantly.

"Hm... yes... so this is what he was studying lately. Hermann Keule: *Über die praktische Verwendung des Nitroglyzerins*; James Brattfield: *About Dynamite*; Böckmann: *Die Explosivstoffe...*"

[9]

THE FURNITURE IN THE STUDY was made of smoke-colored oak. There were deep easy chairs with leather upholstery and smoking tables with copper items and matchboxes in holders. The walls were brown, and the curtains were a slightly darker shade of brown, so not much light could get in.

"This was his *den*," said Mrs. Amsted, "where he could really unwind in the evening with a good book when Leif had been put to bed after his homework was finished."

On the desk was a photograph of Mrs. Amsted and Leif, so that Head Clerk Amsted could always have his family in view even though they might happen to be in one of the other rooms in the apartment. There was an identical photograph on his desk in Section 14 of the War Ministry.

"He always had to have us close to him. His thoughts were always with us."

The detective began his inspection of the desk. He went to work quickly and methodically. It was apparent that he was accustomed to this sort of work and that he would not leave anything in disarray. Mrs. Amsted didn't have to worry.

On top of a blotter with tooled leather corners lay a sheet of paper. The detective immediately recognized the head clerk's meticulous and very legible handwriting. It was evidently the last thing he had written in this life. Or maybe his suicide note was written later?

The detective read through the paper quickly. No. It gave no information about the motive for the head clerk's death.

"... in which instance the directorate must assume the responsibility of non-transference of accounts payable from one fiscal year to the next, inasmuch as the appropriations encumbered each fiscal year for the project in question are allocated in such manner that the procedures employed by the Army's Dirigible Aerodrome, in particular in view of the fact that it is a matter of a not inconsiderable amount of funds, which must of necessity be expected to have an effect on the scope of the measures required *per se,* which in the subsequent fiscal year it will be possible to bring to completion within the Dirigible Aerodrome, insofar as the existing proscription against overexpenditure of allocated monies is to be observed..."

This was apparently work for the Ministry which the head clerk had been busy with in his spare time. It was this work, in his wife's opinion, that he had loved so passionately.

A small account book indicated Mr. Amsted's purely personal expenses: streetcar from the office—20 øre; evening newspaper—10 øre; pack of cheroots—1 krone; paper flower for charity—10 øre. Everything suggested meticulousness and a methodical nature.

In a drawer the detective found rent receipts, a tax assessment form, gas and electric bills, and other receipts. Four lottery tickets—one full coupon and three quarter coupons. Here he also found the policies for fire and theft insurance, for accident insurance, and for the mandatory insurance for domestic help and the laundry woman. So why was the life insurance policy in the crystal bowl on the living room table? Why didn't this orderly man keep it in the drawer along with all the other policies?

But perhaps it was his wife who had moved it. Perhaps she had immediately thought of the life insurance as soon as she heard about her husband's death.

There was a little partitioned box with stamps in it. A bundle of postcards. Stationery and envelopes with lining. There was sealing wax and a signet, and there were unused Christmas cards from the year before.

There was a bronze inkstand and a little brass flagpole and a verdigrised bronze blotter and pewter ashtrays and a silver cigar box and a brass stand to hold pens. And there was a small stuffed dog's foot mounted in silver. It had once been attached to the end of a dachshund's right foreleg—the one it shook hands with. It was a dog his family had owned when he was a boy, and he had grieved so deeply over its death that his father had had the paw stuffed and mounted so that the boy could at least have that as some consolation. Now it was used to brush dirt and eraser crumbs off the writing blotter.

There was a calendar with bridge evenings marked in. There were membership cards to several associations. There was a box with business cards and thumbtacks and paper clips and pencil sharpeners and erasers and penwipers.

There was a paperweight in the shape of a small artillery shell and a letter opener like a miniature sabre. But aside from the paperweight and the scientific works about explosives on the desk, there was nothing that could lead a person's thoughts to death and annihilation or give any explanation for Head Clerk Amsted's bizarre suicide.

The wall cabinet was next. Here were his stamp collection and catalogues and the other philatelic paraphernalia. Here was a bankbook showing 450 kroner and a savings account book showing 2400 kroner and a school savings account book in Leif's name showing 267 kroner and 75 øre. The money for good grades that he had so laboriously saved wound up here. "Someday he'll be glad to have this money, when he's a student at the university. We're bringing him up so he'll know how to *save*. Better to put money in the bank than throw it away on candy and licorice and things like that. And if he promises not to smoke until he's over twenty, he'll get 100 kroner from his father!"

In the cabinet the detective also found the family's certificates: certificate of baptism, certificate of vaccination, certificate of church confirmation, certificate of marriage, and other certificates. And here were Teodor Amsted's diplomas and university matriculation papers and certain important and honorific documents, such as a handwritten note from the Section Chief thanking him for his good wishes on the occasion of his sixtieth birthday.

And there were old letters. Bound neatly with rubber bands. Letters from Mrs. Amsted, written during vacations when separations of several days were unavoidable. Letters concerning Leif's health and behavior. None of them gave the slightest hint of marital complications or anything else that might lead to suicide.

There were photographs in boxes and photographs in albums. Old pictures of the capable members of the Amsted family. Snapshots from vacations and excursions. Leif's first steps. And there were photographs from school, glued to thick cardboard. Of the class, cleverly arranged with a hated teacher in its midst. And the graduation picture of the entire class wearing white graduation caps and white carnations in their buttonholes.

There were old mementos and small souvenirs. Picture postcards from Kullen and the Dybbøl ramparts and Grejsdalen near Vejle. A small shellacked wooden shoe that read "Greetings from Himmelbjerget." A strangely shaped stone. A small piece of amber. Things that were never taken out or looked at, but which, once they were in the cabinet, had to remain there.

Together with the photographs there were several newspaper

clippings. There was, for example, an obituary of Amsted Senior—Section Chief Valdemar Amsted. He must have been just as splendid a person as he was a government official, to judge from the obituary. There were other clippings about his father. Brief notices about decorations he had received, about his seventieth birthday, and about his presence at a royal reception on New Year's Day. They had been cut out of the newspaper in a wonderful show of filial piety and preserved for posterity. Here Leif would be able to read about his grandfather. A rather significant number of newspaper clippings about Teodor Amsted could very likely be collected now. But they probably wouldn't be saved. There was nothing meritorious about being mentioned in that manner.

In fact there was even a clipping concerning Head Clerk Amsted's superior, Section Chief Herluf Ohmfeldt of Section 14 in the War Ministry. It was an article on the occasion of the Section Chief's sixtieth birthday, and there was also a picture of this distinguished government official. But who could possibly have inked in the mustache and glasses? Was it Leif or some other child? Or was it a grown man who had done it absentmindedly? The detective looked a little more closely at it. Across the newsprint someone had written in a refined and elegant hand: "Crook! Crook! Crook!"—over and over. It was Head Clerk Amsted's neat handwriting. No doubt he had done it absentmindedly. But the late head clerk obviously had no love for his boss.

Nothing was disturbed by the detective. He went through everything systematically and expertly. Drawer after drawer. Cabinets and secret compartments. Even the clothing in the wardrobe was inspected. The suits were gray, of the excellent English Chestertown-Deverill quality to which a certain Master Tailor Holm had the exclusive rights. He took along a few buttons for a closer comparison with others that had been found on Amager Common. And the outline of the deceased head clerk's shoes was carefully traced.

The detective jotted things down in his notebook, clearing his throat and nodding meaningfully. But nothing sensational had been found. Nothing had been discovered which in any way might confirm certain theories that the young policeman, quite of his own accord, was toying with.

[10]

THE RED BUILDING on Slotsholm is an unusual place. There is nothing about the exterior of the building that might betray what it is used for. No inscriptions or signs reveal what goes on in the interior of the structure.

The venerable old building is attached to other blocks of buildings, both older and of a more recent vintage, which were originally built separately for vastly different purposes. It is an enormous complex. An entire little city that sits there silent and secretive. A place of tranquility in the center of Copenhagen. A small, quiet, isolated town in the middle of a larger one.

A staggering number of pigeons live on its roofs and cornices. And at certain times during the day they soar up into the air like a cloud when an elderly gentleman shows up carrying a bag of dried peas. When he dies or reaches retirement age, the pigeons will still come flapping down for several more days at the usual time. It will take a little while before they realize that there aren't any more peas for them.

But there are other gentlemen who feed the pigeons at certain other times. And the pigeons will live on and thrive and soil the buildings with their excrement despite the changing generations that come and go.

This place houses Denmark's Central Administration. This is the imperial nerve center. All the powers that keep society functioning radiate from here. This is the residence of *The State*.

On the façade toward Christiansborg Palace hangs a sign: NIGHT BELL FOR THE GENERAL STAFF. If the peace should be broken outside of office hours, the military establishment can be called to arms by a yank on the bell chain.

This is the only sign in the entire complex. There is a multitude of portals and doors, but there are no inscriptions or plaques indicating where they lead. Nor are there any signs, directories, arrows, or pointing hands to serve as orientation in the numerous hallways, courtyards, stairwells, and corridors.

And there don't seem to be any doormen, attendants, or sentries either. The buildings of the Central Administration are open and accessible to everyone. The empire's most precious secrets are protected only by a Yale lock.

In the interior of the building the most perfect silence reigns. Not a sound escapes from the numerous doors. No clattering typewriters. No scraping chairs. No human voices.

A solitary man is walking around inside the building. He wanders down long corridors. He slowly ascends the numerous stairs. He looks probingly at the closed doors. And every once in a while he stops and listens attentively.

The man is wearing a windbreaker and bicycle clips on his pants. He is a detective who is unable to find a certain office. He has been sent here to take statements in connection with Head Clerk Amsted's death. And now he's wasting his time searching. This is an uncomfortable situation for a detective. They would laugh at him back at Police Headquarters if they could see him.

He hears the sound of a door opening. A man comes out into the corridor. The man walks toward him, the first human being the detective has seen in the building.

"Excuse me. I don't suppose you could tell me where Section 14 of the War Ministry is?"

The man stops. He is wearing an alpaca jacket. He must belong in this building. He looks at the detective briefly with strangely vacant eyes. Then he slowly walks on.

"Section 14 of the War Ministry?"

There is no reply. The man walks on without turning around. The detective watches him go.

He continues his search. He knocks on several doors, without getting any answer. He looks down the long corridors, but there is nobody there.

Then it happens again. A door opens, and a man comes out.

"Would you please tell me where Section 14 of the War Ministry is?"

The man doesn't hear the detective. He doesn't see him either. He walks diagonally across the corridor holding a piece of paper in his hand.

"Hello there! Hey! Where's Section 14 of the War Ministry?"

The man goes in through a door on the other side of the hall and closes it behind him.

It's like a bad dream. It's like Odysseus' visit to the Realm of the Shades.

The solitary detective struggles ever onward in the bewitched building. He is on the verge of giving up all hope.

But then another human being appears. A woman is walking down the corridor carrying a pail and a scrub brush. Obviously a cleaning lady. The detective addresses her in a loud voice:

"Do you know where the War Ministry is? I'm trying to find Section 14..."

And this time he gets an answer: "The War Ministry... It's upstairs. All the way up. You'll have to go down the corridor to your left. Then it's the third door on your right."

"Thank you. Thank you. That was *very* kind of you." He gives her a grateful look and hurries on.

No one answers his knock, so he opens the door. He enters a very long room which is partitioned off into stall-like compartments.

In the first stall a man is sitting at a desk looking straight ahead. He appears to be some sort of duty officer. He is wearing an old-fashioned, gold-rimmed pince-nez on a black cord, and he has on a very high wing collar and stiff, loose cuffs that are dangling way down over his hands.

"Hello. Is this Section 14 of the War Ministry?"

No answer.

"I'm from the police. I'm supposed to take some statements in connection with a suicide."

No answer.

"Hello there! Do you hear me? I'm from the police."

There is still no answer.

And now the detective sees that the man is asleep. He is seated in an upright position at his desk, sleeping with his eyes open. It's an art that must have taken him years to perfect.

The detective walks on to the next stall. The man in this one has put his arms on his desk and is resting his head on his arms so that his face cannot be seen. He is sleeping too. But in a more conventional manner.

In the third stall a man is leaning back in his chair with his feet up on his desk. But he is obviously awake. He is reading a book. The detective's sharp eyes note at once that he is reading Stevenson's *Treasure Island*.

"Is this Section 14 of the War Ministry?"

"Yes, what do you want?" The man lowers his book and looks at the detective sullenly. He's the one who is the son of a Royal Privy Council Secretary.

"I'm from the police. I'm looking for some information about Head Clerk Amsted."

"Then you'd better talk to the Section Chief. I'm not authorized to express an opinion on the matter. It's that door over there." The son of the Secretary to the Royal Privy Council resumes reading Stevenson's exciting novel.

[11]

Section Chief Ohmfeldt was sitting at his desk working on a memorandum concerning conditions in the office.

From time to time he composed documents of this nature which he subsequently handed out through the door to the secretary's office. From there the document circulated among the members of the staff, who were supposed to sign their names on the paper as proof that they had read it, after which they were to act in accordance with the instructions given.

After it had circulated, the memorandum was returned through the door to the Section Chief. And after it had been furnished with the date, stamp, and the schedule, file, and registry numbers, the original plus one copy was duly and properly stored away so that, at any given time, coming generations down through the ages would be able to familiarize themselves with the instructions concerning office conditions in Section 14 of the War Ministry which the Section Chief from time to time drew up for his staff.

It had taken the better part of the morning to compose this memorandum. The Section Chief had written numerous outlines and drafts. He was now busy with the final copy.

"During the week now concluded an incident occurred whereby the latch affixed to the topmost window facing onto Slotsholmsgade was not put in operation after opening of said window, in which event said window, in other words, slammed. This same case has arisen, to our knowledge, at least once previously with the result that the aforementioned windowpane was shattered by the uninterrupted slamming motion engendered by the wind, in which event fragments of glass fell onto both the sidewalk and the vehicular traffic lanes. Inasmuch as it must be presumed that all persons employed in this section will endeavor at all times to observe the necessary caution and place the aforesaid device into operation when the conditions for having the window open for one reason or another are deemed to be applicable, I would like to remind you that not only will Section 14 of the War Ministry be encumbered for the expenses pursuant to the fracturing of the glass, but also that the Ministry may under certain circumstances incur liability for compensation pertaining to possible damages or injuries to passersby, be they pedestrian or vehicular in nature, caused by the falling of fragments of glass, in addition to which factors the police regulations governing open windows facing public thoroughfares, squares, or streets must also be borne in mind.

Herluf Ohmfeldt"

The Section Chief was not particularly happy with the visit by the police.

"I was under the impression that I had taken the appropriate measures by telephoning Police Headquarters with regard to the letter posted by Head Clerk Amsted in which notification concerning his peculiar and lamentable suicide was given. Simultaneously this letter was forwarded via registered mail to the police. I fail to see how we in this office might be in a position to provide the police with any information which can further elucidate this regrettable occurrence."

"I would still like to have your permission to ask a few

questions. How was it possible that the letter from Head Clerk Amsted, which was written and mailed the same day that the suicide occurred, was not read until so much later?"

"That is due to the usual business procedures in this office. Under normal circumstances a document addressed to the Ministry would not be read until even later than was the case with the aforementioned letter. That the contents of Head Clerk Amsted's letter nonetheless did become known to me at such an early juncture was due to the fact that the letter was addressed to me personally, for which reason I felt justified in believing that the contents of the letter were of a purely private nature, which also, in point of actual fact, can certainly be said to have been the case."

"But Head Clerk Amsted himself received a letter on the day he left the office for the last time. That is, on the same day he committed suicide. According to what has been reported to the police, that letter arrived at about 2:00 P.M., and the head clerk left the office immediately afterwards. It has further been revealed that this letter obviously threw Head Clerk Amsted into a state of considerable agitation. There is thus reason to assume that receipt of this letter in some way must have had a bearing on his decision to take his own life."

"Yes, there is probably some justification for that assumption."

"But was this letter also subjected to the usual business procedures of this office? I'm asking this because it's important to learn how long a time might have elapsed between the time when the letter was mailed and its receipt by Head Clerk Amsted."

"According to the information that I have received, the aforementioned letter was brought to Mr. Amsted by a messenger — presumably a messenger from a newspaper kiosk. The letter thus did not enter into the Ministry's mail system and was not subjected to the normal clerical procedures but was delivered to

Mr. Amsted personally by the messenger. Not much time can have elapsed, therefore, between dispatch and receipt."

"Thank you, that's a very important piece of information. Now I would simply like to ask you, Section Chief Ohmfeldt, whether anyone here in the Ministry has any idea about what might have been Head Clerk Amsted's motive for this desperate act."

"No. No one has the slightest inkling about his motives."

"What was your impression of Mr. Amsted? Was he nervous and unbalanced? Had he changed recently?"

"No, not at all. Head Clerk Amsted was a calm, self-controlled man."

"How was his relationship with the rest of the office? Was he well liked?"

"Yes, Head Clerk Amsted was well liked and respected by everyone here."

"Weren't there ever any difficulties of any kind? For instance, pertaining to his work?"

"No, absolutely none. There was never any reason to criticize Head Clerk Amsted's work. He was meticulous and dependable in every respect. He was a methodical person. Capable and conscientious. He was a correct and meritorious government official through and through."

"And what did you think of him personally?"

"On a purely personal level I had the very best impression of Head Clerk Amsted. I felt great respect both for him and for his wife. On certain occasions they were guests in my home. I found them both extremely congenial."

"Weren't there ever any frictions of any kind?"

"No, never. I can't remember a single instance in which there was any reason for dissatisfaction with Head Clerk Amsted."

"And did Head Clerk Amsted get along well with his other colleagues?"

"Yes, in my perception the best of relationships prevailed between him and the other people employed in this office."

"And there's no one who has the slightest notion or suspicion about what might have been the cause of his suicide?"

"No, it is completely incomprehensible to all of us here. In my opinion it can only have been a matter of a sudden onslaught of illness. Of mental derangement."

There wasn't much to be learned in Section 14 of the War Ministry. Conversations with the other people in the office shed no light on the event either. Head Clerk Amsted's colleagues were unable to add anything to the Section Chief's information.

"There wasn't anything peculiar about Head Clerk Amsted — not even during his last few days. He was a capable and scrupulous man. No one had anything bad to say about him," said Deputy Clerk Hougaard.

"He was a nice, considerate person. A gentleman. An able and cultivated human being!" said Miss Lilienfeldt.

There had been no frictions. No antagonisms. No jealousies. Nothing that indicated that the deceased might have been unhappy about anything here at the Ministry.

The brown briefcase he had left behind on that fateful day contained only a morning newspaper from the ninth of October and a small box of cheroots. Nor did his desk drawers or cabinet contain anything of interest to the case. There were only papers of a purely official nature.

The head clerk's personal coffee cup and the framed photograph of his wife and son would be sent to his widow along with his briefcase and walking stick.

The only item of significance the detective had obtained from his visit to the red building was the information that the letter which had put Head Clerk Amsted into a state of visible agitation, and which had apparently caused him to leave the office in great haste, had been brought to him by a messenger from a newspaper kiosk.

It was a relatively easy matter for the policeman to find the kiosk from which the letter had been sent. It was the kiosk on Kongens Nytorv. And they were even able to produce the receipt for the letter in Head Clerk Amsted's own handwriting.

The woman at the kiosk who had been on duty on the day in question was even able to remember the person who had delivered the letter to the kiosk. "It was a little boy."

So things were right back where they started. The boy couldn't have been the one who actually sent the letter, of course. His description didn't fit Leif. Besides, Leif was in school at the time anyway. It had quite certainly been a boy picked at random, whom the person who sent the letter had paid to deliver it to the kiosk because he did not wish to be seen himself.

But who was this person?

The young policeman had his own private thoughts on the matter. But they were sheer conjecture which he would certainly be careful not to talk about at Police Headquarters.

[12]

THE POLICE PAID A VISIT to Rosengade as well, to question Mrs. Møller about her lodger — the missing Mikael Mogensen.

"Well, what can I say about him?" she said. "He was a funny one. In a way I suppose he was smarter than most people. He read an awful lot of books in all kinds of languages. I think he was a student once and went to the University. But I guess something snapped inside his head."

The beer merchant in the basement shop said approximately

the same thing when he was asked whether he had known Mikael Mogensen.

"Mogensen... he's all right. He's a fine man. But he's got *bats*!"

"Bats?"

"Yeah, I mean... his lid's on crooked. He says some pretty weird things, you know. Take the other day, for instance: he comes down here to buy a newspaper. And then he says, 'I would like to have the *London Times*. Don't you have the *Times*?'

" 'No,' I says, 'I don't. Won't *Aftenbladet* do, Mr. Mogensen?'

" 'Well, yes, if you don't have anything else. But the English newspapers are really much better than the Danish ones. They are more factual. And they aren't as full of those idiotic sports stories. One does not wish to read about them.'

"So I says to him, 'You don't like sports, Mr. Mogensen?'

" 'No,' he says, 'I regard sports as exceedingly harmful. There are probably a few individually congenial kinds of sports. *Ballooning*, for example. I could very easily imagine myself participating in ballooning if the costs associated with it were not so great. But unfortunately it is a very expensive proposition even to procure the requisite materials.'

"What do you think about that one? Mogensen in a balloon! That's a good one, ain't it?"

"Did Mogensen buy a lot of beer in your store? Or other alcoholic beverages?"

"No, never. Only on the last day he was in here. Then he bought a whole lot of everything. A whole bunch of beer, and schnapps, and port wine. He was having some kind of big bash up in Mrs. Møller's building before he cut out, you see. But ordinarily he only bought newspapers in my place. He didn't even smoke. What do you think happened to him, by the way? Do you think he was the one who blew himself up out on the Common?"

He didn't get an answer. The police don't go in for guessing games.

Mrs. Møller showed the detective Mogensen's room. Everything was still just the way he left it.

"Boy, this is a pretty awful place to live!" he said.

"Awful? What do you mean? For 15 kroner, that I didn't even get? I can't help it that he was such a pig. He didn't want to have the room cleaned. Whenever I came up here to wash the floor, he would say, 'I won't have your ill-timed meddling in my private affairs, Mrs. Møller. You can flaunt your mania for housecleaning down in your own living quarters. I must demand that people leave me in peace here.'"

"But there isn't even a real door here. Anybody can look right through these laths."

"You can't have all the luxuries in the world for 15 kroner, you know."

"Well, no, I suppose you can't. Didn't he have any furniture at all? Where did he sleep?"

"The room was rented to him *unfurnished*. I haven't touched a single thing up here. I don't wish to be accused of that! He slept on the floor. He put newspapers underneath himself. And he used his briefcase as a pillow. I often saw him lying in that position when I came up to the attic with the kitchen lamp. You could see everything through this lath door."

The policeman looked around the room. It was depressing enough to motivate a suicide. The ceiling was so low that a person couldn't even hang himself from it.

"That primus stove actually looks like a real fire hazard. That can't be legal."

"That's not my responsibility. I warned him. I said, 'That piece of junk could blow up and set fire to the entire building.' But it's actually much worse in the room across the hall. That's where the Olsen children sleep, and their parents give them a lighted kerosene lamp to take up with them at night because they're afraid of sleeping in the dark. I call *that* irresponsible. And I've said so hundreds of times to Mrs. Olsen. But what's the use. 'Oh, I'm sure it'll be all right,' she says. 'Nothing's ever happened.' 'No, but some day something'll go wrong!' I tell her."

"Did Mogensen fix his meals up here himself?"

"No, he only made tea. He always drank a tremendous amount of tea. It's a wonder he didn't ruin his stomach."

"Where did he eat?"

"Sometimes he ate over on Klerkegade—in the soup kitchen. But he made a fuss that there was never a single vitamin in the food. I think he mostly hung out at a classy café called 'The Gimmick.' Downtown."

"Oh yes. I know it well."

"I don't understand where he got the money for it. It's always been a mystery to me what he lived on. He didn't get welfare. And I never heard that he had any work. But sometimes he had a lot of money on him."

"There aren't any clothes here. Did he take any baggage when he left?"

"No. He really didn't have any clothes other than the ones he was wearing."

"Yes, but he must have had some . . . some underwear?"

"No. And I've told you that I haven't touched a single one of his things up here! Mogensen pitched his old socks away when he had worn them out. He didn't wear a shirt. Once in a while he bought a shirt-front made out of celluloid or paper, and threw it away when it fell apart."

The detective rooted around in the large pile of newspapers. There really were quite a few issues of the *London Times* among them. At the very bottom of the pile lay several volumes of Louis de Moulin's *Revue*.

He also looked at the books that were stacked up in a corner.

Mogensen's library was a very mixed assortment. At the top of the pile of books lay Colonel Beck's work about Napoleon. Beneath it were several *Rocambole* magazines. Poems by Shelley. *The Three Musketeers*. A murder mystery by Jean Tulipe in French. *Five Weeks in a Balloon* by Jules Verne. *The Anarchist's Bible*. Goldsmith's *History of England, Vol. III*.

And finally some books borrowed from the Royal Library: MacHoowen's *About Dynamite*, Keule: *Nitroglyzerin*. And Böckmann's thick book, *Die Explosivstoffe*.

Mikael Mogensen had apparently been interested in explosives too.

[13]

THE NEWSPAPERS HADN'T WRITTEN as much about Mikael Mogensen's disappearance as they had about Head Clerk Amsted's.

But Mogensen was a human being too. And the police have the same duty to take an interest in his disappearance as in that of an official in a government ministry. And who knows? Maybe there was some sort of connection between the disappearance of the two men after all.

The items in Mogensen's little room are scrutinized and examined just as carefully as Head Clerk Amsted's papers. Each old newspaper is practically turned inside out. The books are leafed through to find possible marginal notes.

Mogensen wasn't a methodical person like Amsted. He didn't have a cabinet on the wall for his papers and old mementos. He didn't have any drawers for his insurance policies and lottery tickets and bankbooks. And he didn't have a wardrobe for his clothes.

He had only the clothes he was wearing. And they were very much the worse for wear. All the clothing that the police can find in his little room is a vest and some discarded celluloid collars. The vest is very dirty. The detective picks it up by two fingers and examines its pockets. They are empty. The vest is made of a gray material. Double-woven wool worsted.

"Does this vest match the suit Mogensen ordinarily wore?"

Yes, Mrs. Møller thinks so. That's exactly the kind of suit he wore. As well as a long, frayed coat.

A closer examination reveals that the dirty vest left behind by Mikael Mogensen was sewn from the same excellent Chestertown-Deverill material which is produced in England and which is sold here in Denmark only by Master Tailor Holm. This is a matter worth noting.

Master Tailor Holm doesn't know Mikael Mogensen. He wasn't one of his customers. There isn't even a Mogensen in his file. And Chestertown-Deverill clothing isn't cheap. It's not the material for a poor man like Mogensen.

But of course Mogensen might have bought his clothing second-hand. Or somebody might have given it to him.

The police ask Mrs. Amsted whether her husband ever knew a person by the name of Mikael Mogensen.

"No," says Mrs. Amsted. "I never heard the name." So her husband can't have known it either. Because he didn't have any secrets from her. And he didn't know anybody on his own. Mrs. Amsted knows this with absolute certainty.

But she doesn't know that among the old mementos in her husband's cabinet there is a photograph of Mikael Mogensen.

She knows that there is a photograph from school in there. A photograph on thick white paper showing little boys cleverly grouped around a teacher with the old linden tree of the Metropolitan School in the background. And she knows that the nice little boy at the far right in the top row is her husband. But Mikael Mogensen had a full beard as an adult. And no detective or wife, no matter how observant they might be, would be able to recognize him as the little boy in that photograph who is kneeling just like the Little Mermaid in the foreground of the picture. He has a sailor suit on. And white knee socks. He is nice and neat. He looks embarrassed because the photographer has placed him in such a ridiculous position. He is well scrubbed with his hair slicked down with water. He doesn't look like the dirty, bearded bohemian from Rosengade. Nevertheless, that's who it is.

It took a long time before the police found out that Teodor Amsted and Mikael Mogensen were classmates. It was due to a chance telephone call from a former teacher who had read in the newspapers about the disappearance of the two men.

Still, there were certain things that attracted the notice of the police right away. There was a common interest in books dealing with explosives. And there was an old vest of fine Chestertown-Deverill material, which Mr. Amsted also used for his suits.

Interrogating the people who had taken part in Mikael Mogensen's farewell bash in Mrs. Møller's building was a difficult job. By and large they were people who had some unfinished business with the police and who as a result were not easy to find at home. And when someone finally was found, the person in question was not terribly inclined to say much. They were people who had been interrogated by the police before and knew how to wriggle around questions.

The detective managed to have a talk with Peter the Soldier, a small-time thug who got high on wood alcohol and fruit juice. The detective wasn't able to drag too many words out of the Soldier. Mrs. Olsen from the basement ice cream store was only able to tell him about the quarrel with Mrs. Møller. "It was something else." A boatman who rowed provisions out to the vessels at the lime-kiln harbor told them that Mogensen had been intoxicated. And the boatman, who had been to sea and understood English, told how Mogensen in his drunkenness had mainly spoken English, to the great displeasure of the linguistically inferior Mrs. Møller. "I am the last humanist in Europe!" he had repeated over and over. "One of the noblest figures in our history will die with me!"

Perhaps these strange words indicated that Mogensen was thinking about dying.

[14]

Mrs. Amsted had decided that her husband should have a quiet funeral due to the unusual nature of his demise. And that was what the death notice said.

It had not been easy to formulate a death notice under these circumstances. She had always thought that when her husband died, the death notice would say that he had "passed away peacefully and quietly." But this phrase could not be used under the present conditions.

It cost her a great deal of thought before she succeeded in composing a satisfactory announcement.

> *My beloved husband, our little son's dear father, Head Clerk in the War Ministry*
>
> TEODOR AMSTED
>
> *died suddenly without any preceding illness. The funeral will be private.*

As soon as the Institute of Forensic Medicine had concluded its examination and released the remains of the deceased, the coffin was taken out to the chapel at Assistens Cemetery. Then a man from the funeral parlor came to call at the apartment on Herluf Trollesgade to determine what arrangements Mrs. Amsted wished to have made for the funeral.

He was a short, gaunt man with black gloves and a mournful and sympathetic face. Mrs. Amsted liked him. She sensed that he understood her grief and that he was ready to do everything to spare her from any unnecessary inconvenience.

"I want it to be private. Just Leif and myself and those nearest and dearest to us."

"Oh yes, I quite understand. But what about the singing? We provide the singing as well. Which hymns do you wish to have sung?"

"I haven't even thought about that yet. What do people usually . . . ? Oh yes, I think we should have the one with, 'None knows the day till the sun has set.' Oh, what's it called now?"

" 'Blissful, Blissful'!"

"Yes, that one. And then 'Churchbell, Not for the Big Cities But for the Little Town Were You Cast' — it's so pretty. We sang it at my father's funeral too. It's practically a family tradition. My husband was quite fond of it too."

"Yes, it *is* beautiful. Just let me jot that down: 'Churchbell Not for . . .' "

"Isn't that enough?"

"Well, people *do* usually have three. That's the most common number. What would you say to 'Wondrous Is the Earth' as the coffin is being carried out, Mrs. Amsted? People frequently use that one."

"Yes, that one as the final one then. But then those three will do. It will be beautiful. He would have liked it."

"And the choir? You'll almost have to have somebody to do the singing, you know. Ten voices cost 30 kroner. But of course you can get by with fewer too. You can go all the way down to two voices — for 7 kroner."

"Isn't there something in between?"

"Oh yes. Six voices — 20 kroner. Eight voices — 25 kroner."

"I think we should take the eight voices."

"Very good. Eight voices. Now what about the candelabras?"

"Candelabras?"

"Yes, two candelabras at the coffin are the rule at a standard funeral. But of course it *does* look much better with *four*, I must say. One at each corner of the coffin. Extra candelabras cost 3 kroner apiece."

"All right, let's have the two extra ones then. The first two are included in the price, aren't they?"

"Yes. And then there's the side lighting. Side lighting in the chapel costs 8 kroner. Do you want the side lighting lit?"

"Is it necessary?"

"It *is* rather dark in the chapel, you know."

"I see. Then it would be best to have the side lighting too. Let's not try to economize for the sake of 8 kroner."

"It *is* more congenial when the side lighting is lit. I do have to admit that. What about the trees?"

"What trees?"

"The laurel trees. They cost 1.50 apiece. Trees are *not* included in the price of a standard funeral."

"But laurel trees... aren't those the kind they put in tubs? Outside of bars, I mean?"

"Not entirely the same kind. These are more elongated. More like cypress trees. It does look more *festive* with trees, you know, three on each side, for example — for a total of six in all."

"Good. Let's have the trees then. Now, is there anything else?"

"I imagine you'll want the carpet rolled out?"

"What carpet is that?"

"The carpet for the chapel floor. It costs 4 kroner to have it rolled out. Otherwise it will stay rolled up."

"If people usually have the carpet, then just leave it. Now, there can't be anything else, can there?"

"Not too much more, Mrs. Amsted. We do have to have pallbearers, of course."

"But won't friends be carrying the coffin out?"

"Yes, but they can only carry it out of the chapel. The pallbearers will be waiting outside. Very often it's a long way from the chapel to the gravesite, you know. You can see here in the regulations, Mrs. Amsted. Pallbearers are *mandatory*. And in this instance, where it's a double coffin, we can't use fewer than eight men. You can see, Mrs. Amsted—it says so right here. It's 10 kroner per man."

"Well, I guess that's the way it has to be. To think that eight men are really necessary!"

"It's the law, Mrs. Amsted."

"Oh, I know—but that really is an awful lot!"

"Then there are the decorations for the coffin. How much had you thought of spending, Mrs. Amsted?"

"Flowers for the coffin have been arranged. I've spoken with a florist."

"I see, yes. So, *no* decorations for the coffin. *We* could have taken care of that easily enough."

"But it's *been* taken care of."

"Yes, of course—I mean, just for future reference."

The undertaker looked through his list again and tallied it up. Everything seemed to be in order and added up. He stuck the papers in his pocket and stood up with his hat in his hand.

"Well, there isn't anything else. Goodbye, then, Mrs. Amsted. Everything will be done to your satisfaction. You'll find that it will be *beautiful*!... You won't see me until we're out there. I'll come out to the chapel in plenty of time and accept the wreaths and flowers and take care of whatever else there might be. We'll lay the wreaths out away from the coffin, as they arrive—in sort of a cross shape. You mustn't worry about a thing, Mrs. Amsted. Everything will work out just fine."

The undertaker was a dependable and tactful man. He arrived at the chapel wearing a high silk hat and black gloves twenty minutes before the funeral was scheduled to begin. From time to time he glanced surreptitiously at a small piece of paper that he held in his hand and surveyed the entire scene.

He carefully arranged the wreaths that had already arrived in the manner indicated. And he personally accepted new wreaths brought by various delivery boys.

There were many wreaths from family and friends.

Flowers from his colleagues at the War Ministry also arrived at Head Clerk Amsted's bier. The office *per se* was unable to make any official show of sympathy. But on a purely private basis the employees had sent beautiful wreaths and decorations. Flowers came from the Section Chief too, and this touched Mrs. Amsted deeply.

Head Clerk Degerstrøm, who now stood next in line for promotion when the Section Chief finally attained an appropriate age, showed up in person. He nurtured warm and grateful feelings for the deceased. And he clasped the widow's hand firmly. Miss Lilienfeldt from the office showed up too. She thought funerals were beautiful. She was a sensitive soul who shared other people's grief. She cried so much she shook all over.

Despite the announced privacy, a newspaper had dispatched its special funeral correspondent to the chapel.

"The funeral was held yesterday for Head Clerk Amsted, whose ghastly death on Amager Common made a profound and harrowing impression on the public mind.

"In the cold autumn weather a small cortège gathered at the bier of the pulverized head clerk in the chapel at Assistens Cemetery, Mrs. Amsted in deep mourning, with her son Leif, 13, by her side. Only the family and closest friends were present. It was a small, profoundly moved circle of people seated around the coffin in the large chapel.

"Pastor Olsen from Garnison Church spoke beautifully and movingly from the psalm, 'None knows the day till the sun has set.' 'Judge not,' said the pastor, 'lest ye be judged! No one knows what feelings agitated this man's heart during the final, bitter hours of his life. But we do know that he was a good husband and father.'

"Then Grundtvig's beautiful hymn was sung: 'Churchbell, Not for the Big Cities But for the Little Town Were You Cast.' 'He went away like unto the setting of the harvest sun,' the last line says. What could have been more appropriate?

"Friends carried the coffin from the chapel to the strains of 'Wondrous Is the Earth.' Some people seemed to be thinking that the coffin was conspicuously light.

"The pastor's three shovelfuls of earth made a hollow sound on the nearly empty coffin.

"The widow's tears fell onto the grass."

[15]

Mrs. Amsted continued to live in the apartment on Herluf Trollesgade.

"For Leif's sake. Leif and I will preserve the old home. Everything will remain just as it was, and the way *he* liked it. Leif must not forget his dear father."

Now whenever Leif didn't want to clean his plate, he was confronted with what his father would have thought. "What do you think Papa would say now if he knew you were leaving something on the edge of your plate again?" In tears and weighed down by a guilty conscience, Leif would have to eat those last clammy fish balls and celery.

This applied to his homework and his German composition and his math assignments on Thursday nights. "Think of your father, Leif! Think about what he would have said. Do you think he would have been happy that you waited until the last minute *again*?"

The spirit of the deceased lived on in the home on Herluf Trollesgade. Somehow it hadn't made such a terribly great difference that he was dead. In a way his personality made more of an impression on his home now than it did when he was alive. He seemed to have more influence. "What would Father have said about that?" Or: "No, Father wouldn't have liked that!" And: "You know it would make your father happy!"

Before, when there was something Leif wasn't allowed to do, Mrs. Amsted would always say, "No. Father says no!" Then she would call in to her husband in his study, "Isn't that right?" "Yes, of course!" he would reply, even though he didn't know what it was all about. And it was still that way. "*Father* would certainly say no!" was the way it went now.

In Teodor Amsted's case, it was of no particular significance that he was dead. It made essentially no difference whether he himself was sitting in his armchair or whether his photograph was standing on the card table.

He provided for his family after his death too. Every month his pension was paid out to Mrs. Amsted. It had always been one of his goals to get a pension. Even beside his cradle people had said he should become something that entitled him to a pension when he was 65. The pension had been the main purpose of his life, so to speak. And now the pension was paid out regularly, even though he was only 46 when he died.

But he looked after his family in another way as well. Mrs.

Amsted had a rather substantial sum of money from life insurance paid out to her. The life insurance policy had been taken out as soon as they were married. Right after he had received his law degree. It had not been done in vain. It stood the family in good stead now. "He would have been pleased about it now," said Mrs. Amsted.

Mrs. Amsted and Leif had no need to fear for their wellbeing. They were financially secure. And at the same time they also had four chances for a sudden and unexpected increase in their fortune.

The head clerk had left behind four tickets to the state lottery — one whole ticket and three quarter tickets. The tickets had been faithfully renewed throughout all the years they had been married. Every so often one of them would win 30 kroner. But the possibility for those 240,000 kroner was still there.

In actuality there had been *five* tickets. But one of them had vanished with Head Clerk Amsted.

Mrs. Amsted had searched for it everywhere. It was a half ticket which her husband had inherited from his parents. It hadn't won anything in living memory, so it was probably due for something big soon. But it was gone now. The other four tickets were renewed and lay neatly in the usual desk drawer, but the fifth one was missing. And it was precisely this ticket that was the family's favorite one. Perhaps precisely because of its obstinacy — its number never came up.

Possibly Mr. Amsted had had it in his pocket on that fateful day when he died, and the ticket had been destroyed with him. But why would he be walking around with it in his pocket? That wasn't like him. Why had it been separated from the other four tickets in the desk drawer? It was one more mystery among all the other mysteries.

His stamp collection was still in the wall closet beside his desk. And the various instruments that Teodor Amsted had used in arranging and mounting the stamps were still on the same shelf. A magnifying glass and tongs and a perforation gauge and watermark detector and stamp hinges and a thick catalogue from Switzerland.

Leif cast covetous glances at these items. He wanted to get on with the work. But the things were untouchable now. "When you grow up, this will all be yours. Then you can continue your father's work. And believe me, the stamps will be valuable then. But *now* you mustn't touch anything. What do you think Father would say if he saw you? His stamps! His most precious possessions! No, no, Leif! Out of the question! Father would never give you his permission!"

They went out to the cemetery regularly, Leif and the black-clad Mrs. Amsted. And they stood there by the grave, not really knowing what to do. They couldn't just leave right away, of course, walk all the way out to Assistens Cemetery and then turn around and walk home.

So they stood out there feeling slightly cold in the chill autumn breeze. There wasn't anything to fuss over at the grave yet. The numerous wreaths were lying on top of the yellow clay mound. The grave couldn't be put in order until later.

"But after the grave has been fixed up, then we'll make sure to take care of it," said Mrs. Amsted. "Then we'll water the flowers and rake the dirt out here. Things will always look nice on Papa's grave."

Leif was cold. And he shuddered as he thought of the coffin that was lying down there in the brown clay soil. He thought of the coffins he had seen in the display windows of the casket stores. White coffins with padding and pillows. Open, inviting you to lie right down in them.

And he thought of the strange way his father had died and wondered what could possibly be left of him.

His mother felt he had too much imagination. It distracted him. When he thought about too many things, he couldn't concentrate on his homework. And that was what counted. But the principal had said there was no harm in it. So many children had imaginations and thought of lots of things. But it would die down. The school would see to that. There was no reason to worry. He was sure it would pass. It always did.

Maybe his father had had an imagination once, and stuff like that. But he'd gotten over it. Still, it was strange the way he had died. You would have to have imagination to think of doing that.

Leif was thinking. He couldn't talk to his mother about it. She didn't even think he knew anything about it. But maybe she was thinking about the same thing.

"You must never forget your father, Leif. When you grow up, you must be just like he was. Just as orderly and capable and decent. Do you hear me?"

Leif nodded.

"And if anybody says anything ugly about your father, you must never believe it! Never!"

They had reached Kapelvej, where there are nothing but flower shops and casket stores. You could borrow small trowels and rakes from the flower shops. In the casket stores the coffins were standing open. Padded and white and inviting. Ready to climb into.

Only on the corner of Nørrebrogade was there a different kind of store. A fun little shop with accordions and music boxes and musical instruments. But Leif didn't really feel that it would look right for him to stop there and revel in these things. When you were walking home from the cemetery, your mood was supposed to be somber.

It was raining, and the wind snatched at Mrs. Amsted's mourning veil. She had trouble controlling it, and her umbrella too. "Now we'll have to get the grave fixed up nicely. Tomorrow I'll go to the cemetery office and let them know. And we'll have to get a stone for the grave too. A beautiful, simple stone that Father would have liked."

On the other side of Queen Louise's Bridge they went into a bakery and bought pastries to take home for their afternoon tea. Two croissants and two filled with custard. "Papa was so fond of those."

[16]

TEODOR AMSTED'S SPIRIT lived on.

It lived on not only in his home on Herluf Trollesgade. Not only in his apartment where his photograph in its leather frame stood on the shiny table looking anxiously at Leif. Leif had a very guilty conscience when their eyes met.

It wasn't because his father's look was stern. If anything, Teodor Amsted had been a little bashful about peering into the photographer's camera while his head was bathed in the blinding spotlight, which produced peculiar shadows on his face.

He had a couple of worried wrinkles on his forehead. His eyes were pale blue and rather tired, his mouth smiling a little shyly. But you couldn't really see his mouth because of the little English mustache that cast deep shadows under the adroit lighting of the photographer.

Here, then, was the deceased head clerk, taking an active part in the life of his family. He had more to say now than when he was alive. He made decisions and resolved problems and settled disputes. He sat there in his leather frame gazing out into the living room and took part in everything.

Teodor Amsted's spirit lived on. It also lived on in another and more independent way than anyone could have imagined. Mysterious and unheard-of things began to happen.

These strange and wonderful things came to Mrs. Amsted's

attention thanks to a lady she didn't know. Or in any case a lady who was *almost* a stranger. A lady whom the Amsted family had met by chance at a seaside *pension* many years before. Since then they hadn't had any contact with her. It was a very brief summer acquaintance. But Mrs. Amsted remembered her well.

She was an author. A unique and very interesting lady with black hair and green earrings and exotic fringes on her sleeves. Her name was Sylvia Drusse.

"Oh, how very nice of you to look us up in our solitude, Mrs. Drusse! Yes, of course—I recognized you immediately. I haven't forgotten you. Oh, what a long, long time it's been. How far away it all seems. That was back when everything was different... To think that you still remember us!"

"It is in times of need—and *grief*—that people should remember their friends." Mrs. Drusse extended her arms and took Mrs. Amsted by the shoulders. "Dear, dear little Mrs. Amsted... how much you've had to go through! Oh, how I do understand you! When you yourself have lost the one you love, then you also understand the loss of others."

Mrs. Amsted wept. Mrs. Drusse led her over to a chair and had her take a seat. Mrs. Drusse had in a sense become the hostess.

"Go ahead and cry... go ahead. It's a good thing to cry it all out. Believe me, I know all about crying."

Mrs. Amsted sobbed.

"And what a beautiful home you have, Mrs. Amsted! Do you keep house yourself, you busy little thing?"

"I have a young maid to help me. There's Leif to take care of too, of course."

"Yes, certainly. Oh, I can remember when *my* boy was little. How much there was to do! And I was writing at the same time. Goodness, I had to manage it all by myself. But a *mother* finds time for everything... Now he's grown up. He's in America. I hear from him only occasionally, in fact. When they grow up and fly away, they forget what their mother meant to them. You'll find that out too someday, dear Mrs. Amsted."

"Leif is so affectionate. He has his father's kind, affectionate disposition."

"Ah yes, *Leif* — that's what his name was. I remember him so well. The way he played in the sand with his little scoop and pail. Ah yes — what a beach — it was an entire world for his little child's imagination. A big, rich, and radiant world!" Mrs. Drusse flung her arms wide so the fringes on her sleeves fluttered.

"I remember you and your husband and Leif so well. You were the only really cultivated people in the *pension*. So many plebeians come to places like that. People who only have a short vacation and who have saved up all year to play the aristocrat for a single week. Ah yes — vanity! Vanity!"

"Yes, I do recall that the patronage in that *pension* wasn't really very high-class... Perhaps that's why we got together, Mrs. Drusse. Oh, I think it's just so touching that you thought of us and stopped by."

"It's nothing, dear Mrs. Amsted. We're happiest when we live for others. The more we forget ourselves, the closer we come to what we call happiness. That is the wisdom I've acquired in my life."

Mrs. Drusse had taken her hand and now sat patting it. Some time elapsed, during which they did not speak. Mrs. Drusse looked around the room.

"That hortensia does look pretty there! Of course you remember that it must only be watered in its saucer. It needs a lot of water, but never in the pot itself. Only in the saucer."

Mrs. Drusse, the author, answered questions from the readers in the letters column of *Home Journal*. She knew everything about potted plants and moth remedies and blackheads and graphology and compounds for removing spots from clothing.

On the table was some needlework that Mrs. Amsted had put down when the doorbell rang.

"Oh, may I see it? Is this something busy little Mrs. Amsted is sewing herself? My, what pretty embroidery! Pearl cotton, isn't it? Wonderfully vibrant colors! I love colors. They mean so much for our psyche. And for our physical well-being too. You can cure diseases with colors."

"Is that really possible?"

"Yes. It's something that was known even in antiquity. The ancients knew much more than we do. Of course, 'science' thinks it knows everything. *Science,* hah! No, the ancients knew. The wisdom of Egypt. The mysticism of the Orient. *Atlantis!* There's more between heaven and earth than 'science' suspects."

"Yes, I'm sure there is. But now let me make you a cup of tea, Mrs. Drusse. All right?"

"Yes, thank you — a nice cup of hot tea would do me good. I love tea. But let me help you, dear Mrs. Amsted!"

"No, no, Mrs. Drusse. Just sit right there."

"All right, since you absolutely insist. But ordinarily I'm not accustomed to being waited on."

They had cookies with their tea. Vanilla wafers and the like.

"These taste delightful. Did you bake them yourself? You must give me the recipe, Mrs. Amsted!"

"No, I didn't bake them myself. But they *are* more or less home-made. They're from Karen's Home Bakery on Bredgade. I think their things always taste so good."

"They're wonderful!" Mrs. Drusse ate with surprising gusto. "I was actually so sure you had baked them yourself. You're really such an industrious little housewife, standing in your little kitchen baking and frying and keeping everything sparkling clean! Oh, this is wonderful tea. I can tell that you know about tea. One should bring the water to a roaring boil and pour it into the pot right away. So many people let the water sit there and boil too long. Or forget to warm up the teapot first."

"Yes, I'm very fond of good tea. I was in London when I was young. I learned how to make tea there, the way it's supposed to be made. The English never use a tea strainer."

"No. Never." Mrs. Drusse knew that too.

"My husband preferred coffee. In the beginning, that is. But he acquired a taste for tea. Coffee was the only thing we didn't agree on. Otherwise we had the same taste in absolutely everything."

"Yes, that was something I even noticed back at the summer *pension*. 'This is an unusually harmonious marriage,' I said to myself. 'These two people have the spiritual contact required for harmony and what we call happiness.' "

"Yes, I believe we did. There were so many times when I would suggest something to my husband and he had just thought of the same thing. Or when I would ask him to do something, and he had already done it. It was just as if I always knew what he was thinking."

"Yes, yes. That's the way it is. It's the spiritual contact between two people. I always suspected that it existed between you and your husband. I suppose I might even say that's actually why I came here to see you."

"Pardon me? I don't really understand you, Mrs. Drusse."

"I have a *message* for you!"

[17]

"A MESSAGE?"

"Yes." Mrs. Drusse was silent for a long time. She had closed her eyes halfway. It was as if she were gazing at something far away. Something that was hidden from other people.

"Do you know the book about *Raymond*, Mrs. Amsted?"

"No, what sort of book is that?"

"It's called *Raymond Lives*. The famous English scientist, Sir Oliver Lodge, wrote it. It's about his son. His only son who was killed in the war. Sir Oliver Lodge obtained *evidence* that Raymond was alive. That he was living in another world. A world that resembles our own in many ways, but a *purer* world. A richer and more beautiful world. And what is more, Sir Oliver established contact with his son. He received messages from him. They exchanged thoughts. They spoke to each other."

"I think that sounds almost spooky, Mrs. Drusse."

"No, no, my dear. It's not spooky. Is it spooky to know that our loved ones are alive? Is it spooky to speak with those we have loved? No, no."

"I've never heard of anything like that before, Mrs. Drusse. It's so foreign to me."

"You must remember that Sir Oliver Lodge was a *scientist*. He was of a critical and skeptical frame of mind. But he became convinced. And he made it his life's work to let other people share what he had experienced. He has contributed to removing the terror of death from humanity!"

"I'd like very much to read his book."

"I've brought it along for you. You must read it at once. Oh, it's a book that's more beautiful and rich and intelligent than any other!"

"I look forward very much to reading it. It was nice of you to bring it along for me."

"You'll love this book. It's so true and convincing. Remember, he's a scientist. Everything took place under the strictest *scientific* control."

"Do you really think that the dead are alive? I don't mean in the way religion teaches us — but in some kind of direct way — so that they can see and hear what we're doing?"

"I don't think it. I *know* it. I have experienced it myself. I have talked with the so-called 'dead' just the way I'm sitting here talking to you."

"It's so strange, Mrs. Drusse..."

Teodor Amsted's photograph gazed out into the living room.

He had a couple of worried wrinkles on his forehead. And he was smiling rather shyly.

"You know, now that you've told me about all this, Mrs. Drusse—it really has seemed as if he has been here in the living room with us—with Leif and me. I've often felt that way. It's been so strange."

The light in the living room had gradually grown dim. Mrs. Drusse sat holding her friend's hand. She was speaking very softly to her. Slowly and softly.

A new and wonderful world was opening up to Mrs. Amsted. These were things she had never heard of before. Life on various planes of existence. Life that was completely different from life on earth, and yet resembled it in some respects. Flowers, for example, also grew on the other plane of existence. And these flowers had fragrances. And with the help of a medium the so-called 'living beings' here on the earthly plane could also experience these fragrances. Mrs. Drusse herself had once distinctly smelled the fragrance of lilies of the valley and violets. And this was in the middle of winter when those kinds of flowers don't even grow.

The fascinating thing about it was that Mrs. Drusse had been through it all herself. She had had a young friend—an artist—who had died abroad. And she had spoken with him. She had learned about his existence on the other plane. He had helped her and given her advice.

She had also spoken with her husband. The late Mr. Drusse had been an actor here on earth. And he also practiced his art on the other plane. There was theater in the spiritual world too. But completely different from here. It was like a kind of worship service. But they also performed works by the great earthly writers. On the spiritual plane Mr. Drusse had played all the classical roles that he had never had the chance to play here on the earthly plane.

It was mysterious and wonderful.

This visit was of great significance to Mrs. Amsted. It was decisive for her entire existence. It gave her life a direction and a meaning that she had never dreamed of.

[18]

A SMALL CIRCLE OF PEOPLE gathered in a villa out in Valby.

These were people whose thoughts were preoccupied with a different world from this one and a different life from the earthly life. They called each other Brother and Sister. And the villa where they held their meetings and seances they called the Temple of Solomon.

They looked like any other people. They wore ordinary clothing, and hats and raincoats. They had their own businesses and occupations here on earth. There was a printer and a traveling salesman and a woman who owned an ice cream store. They earned their money and paid their rent and ate their food just like other people. But their spirits were turned toward the infinity of the universe. Their thoughts were occupied by the eternal mysteries. Their souls moved in regions which ordinary mortals knew nothing about.

Mrs. Amsted felt slightly uneasy toward these Brothers and Sisters she didn't know. When the red seance lamp was lit, she would stick close beside Mrs. Drusse. And Mrs. Drusse would hold her hand and whisper, "Don't be afraid. Don't be afraid, little Sister. You just have to *concentrate* as hard as you can." But Mrs. Amsted didn't really know what she was supposed to concentrate on.

Amazing things went on in the Temple of Solomon. The peculiarly constructed three-legged table was the material instrument through which the spirits of the dead could communicate. Soft music was played on a reed organ. It wasn't simply because the spirits liked music. It was also to make it easier for the medium to go into the trance which made it possible for the other life-forms to take up temporary residence in his corporeal substance. His name was Olsen. He was a tall young man with a pretty face. He was delicate and slightly effeminate. He would be totally drained after a seance, but the other Sisters and Brothers were kind to him and helped him in every way.

It was Mrs. Drusse who made the greatest use of this connecting link to the invisible, spiritual world. And several of the Sisters grumbled about her: "Why should she be the one to do it all the time? The rest of us would like to have a chance too!" They were like people waiting outside a telephone booth who get impatient because one person ties up the phone too long.

They did have to admit, however, that for the sake of psychic research Mrs. Drusse's seances were the most interesting.

She had a special ability to establish contact quickly with the deceased young artist who had also been close to her on the earthly plane.

"Is that you, Hakon?" she would ask in a soft voice. And the yes-leg of the table would tap.

"How are you?"

"F-i-n-e," tapped the table leg. And one of the Brothers would write down the letters. Lengthy conversations could be carried on in this way. And sometimes they were of such an intimate nature that several of the Sisters were shocked. And one time the leader of the circle, Damascus the printer, even had to call Hakon to order.

But the most interesting thing was that right in the middle of the conversation a second spirit might appear and disrupt the proceedings.

When Hakon tapped with the yes-leg, the second spirit tapped violently with the no-leg. This could assume the dimensions of a furious quarrel. The medium suffered a great deal from this. The spirits almost seemed to be ripping and tearing at his body. He moaned and groaned in the most heart-rending manner.

At first they had thought that this disruptive spirit was one of the so-called mischievous spirits who not infrequently appear at seances and disturb the communications of the more serious spirits. But it soon proved to be none other than Mrs. Drusse's late husband putting in his two cents' worth.

"Wait, please! Wait!" the printer Damascus would shout. "One at a time!" But nothing could stop Mr. Drusse.

They tried using another, larger table, and both spirits made themselves known by talking at the same time. Mrs. Drusse said that her husband had always been unreasonably jealous on the earthly plane too. She had hoped it would subside after his death, now that anything other than a pure and platonic relationship was out of the question. But no, Mr. Drusse's spirit could go totally berserk. And Hakon, who was a very impulsive sort, would give it right back to him in no uncertain terms.

Sometimes the large table would tap with two legs at a time. The wood creaked, and the legs threatened to snap off. The movements of the table would get so violent that the circle of Brothers and Sisters maintaining the contact would be hard pressed to keep up with it. The table virtually tramped around the room.

"Yes—yes!" tapped Hakon.

"No! No! No!" thundered Mr. Drusse.

It was harrowing and tremendously strenuous. The circle had to stand up in order to follow the table's movements. Brothers and Sisters had to scurry around the room to keep up with it. The sweat poured off them. It was a terrible effort.

Once during a violent struggle between the two rival spirits, the table turned completely around so that the participants in the circle almost fell down. The table thundered around the room and slammed abruptly into the door. At the suggestion of one of the Brothers the door was opened, and the table rushed into the adjoining room, where it crashed into the walls and the other furniture. The sweating and exhausted participants literally had to chase down the obstreperous table.

"Oh God! Oh God!" cried Mrs. Drusse. "They'll murder each other! They're so passionate, both of them. So fiery and wild! . . . They'll kill each other!"

"They could never do that, you know. Even if they wanted to," Damascus the printer reassured her.

"Oh, that's the way it was when they were on earth too. They have such proud and unyielding temperaments. They're such resolute and fiery men. How is this going to end!"

Then the table stopped, because it broke apart. Mr. Drusse's no-leg had fallen off.

The dead-tired medium lost consciousness. For a while they feared for his life, it took such a long time for him to come around again.

For some time they had to discontinue the seances, and Mrs. Drusse was enjoined to make her husband control himself. Otherwise they wouldn't dare establish any contact.

[19]

MRS. AMSTED DID NOT manage to make direct contact with her husband right away.

"That's always the way it is," they told her. It took some time for the spirits to settle in on the other plane. But there were spirits who looked after the new arrivals. A sort of guardian or attendant spirit. And through them one could receive communications concerning the recently deceased.

The name of Teodor Amsted's attendant spirit was Helmuth Zögerer. He had been a professor at the University of Graz when he was alive and appeared to be a gifted and cultivated man. Teodor Amsted was in the best of hands.

"*Guten Abend, Herr Professor!*" said Damascus the printer when Olsen's trance had commenced and contact had been established.

"*Wie geht es unserem Freund, Teodor Amsted?*"

"*G-u-t*," tapped the table leg.

"He's fine," the printer told Mrs. Amsted.

"Tell him that his wife is sitting here in our circle," Damascus said to Professor Zögerer.

The yes-leg tapped.

"Does he already know?"

"Yes."

"Can he put in an appearance himself?"

A knock from the no-leg.

"I see, not yet. When?"

"L-a-t-e-r."

"Thank you, Herr Professor. Teodor Amsted's wife would like to ask a few questions now. Is that permissible?"

"Yes."

"Is he all right?" asked Mrs. Amsted in a soft voice.

"Yes."

And then suddenly it seemed that she couldn't think of anything more to ask. And the professor from Graz grew impatient and withdrew.

But eventually she became more accustomed to seances. And the moment finally arrived when Teodor Amsted himself made an appearance. Control experiments were undertaken to ascertain that it really was him and not some mischievous spirit. He was asked about things which only he could be presumed to know. And he answered satisfactorily.

He was able to answer correctly the question about how many

cheroots there were in a specific box. He could count to the street number of their building on Herluf Trollesgade. And the table's counting leg tapped 46 times when he was asked how many years he had lived on the earthly plane.

"Why did you do it?" Mrs. Amsted asked him in a quavering voice.

But the table remained silent. It was obviously a question that could not yet be answered.

However, he was able to give some information about the purely external living conditions on the spiritual plane. It was beautiful where he was. Much more beautiful than on earth. You wouldn't be able to imagine it.

"Are you getting the right things to eat?"

"No."

"The spirits don't eat at all. They have no need of it!" one member of the circle informed her.

"What about clothes?"

"The Sister must ask more directly!" the leader of the circle interrupted.

"Do you wear clothes?"

"Yes."

"What are your clothes like?"

"W-h-i-t-e."

"What do you do over there? Do you have anything you're working on?"

"No."

"It always takes a little while before the spirits get the work they're suited for. First they have to settle in on the other plane," the printer informed her.

To the question, "Who wrote the letter you received at the office?" there was no answer.

"Try something he can answer yes or no to," said Damascus.

"Was it a woman who wrote it?"

"No."

"Was it a man?"

"Yes."

This answer greatly reassured Mrs. Amsted. This was the problem that was still tormenting her. She knew that the spirits could not lie. And she knew that her husband couldn't lie to her. She felt the satisfaction of having regained control over her husband.

Mrs. Amsted never established a close personal relationship with the other Sisters and Brothers of the circle. It was as if these people were too distant from her on a purely social basis. She did not possess the ability of the poet, Mrs. Drusse, to adapt herself to various sorts of people.

Only with the medium did she come to be on rather intimate terms. Between Mrs. Amsted and delicate, young Olsen with his pretty face there arose an empathy which could be interpreted as spiritual affinity and harmony. For Mrs. Amsted, Olsen was the true intermediary of the contact with her husband, the man to whom she had meant everything and who had developed under her influence.

[20]

THERE WERE PLENTY of people who were preoccupied with Head Clerk Amsted.

But the missing Mikael Mogensen was not forgotten either. There were people who were worried about him as well.

Admittedly, there wasn't any photograph of him in a leather frame anywhere. He didn't have any children either, who were supposed to grow up and be just like him. And there was no circle of Sisters and Brothers who met in the light of a red lamp to conjure up his spirit from the other world.

He had no next of kin who were interested in him or were so closely related to him that they needed to mourn him. He had been a solitary man.

But when he disappears, society is just as interested in him as in its other members. He had the same duty as everyone else to be entered in the national registry and to register for the draft and to report any change of address and to pay his taxes. And when he turns up missing, it is society's duty to find him. When he dies, society must determine what he died of. In this case there is no difference between rich and poor.

When people are alive, they are free to decide for themselves what they want to eat, or whether they want to eat, or whether they can earn enough to get anything to eat. But when they die, the State steps in and demands that a cause of death be established, and it requires a proper death certificate. And if a person disappears, the same investigative apparatus is set in motion to find him, regardless of whether he is rich and famous or poor and unknown.

There are several thousand people walking around who don't have enough to eat and don't have decent clothes on and don't have any place to sleep. If they don't do anything illegal, society doesn't worry about them. But if one of them asks somebody for 25 øre for a night's lodging, a fully equipped police car will roar out of the station and arrest him. A district attorney will bring him before the bench. A lawyer will defend him. A judge will convict him. A host of prison guards will guard him. Prosecuting his breach of the law is not cheap.

A man is allowed to starve himself to death. But if he jumps into the harbor and drowns, no means will be spared to recover his body. The police and rescue corps, divers and aircraft will be brought into action. No expense is too great.

Mikael Mogensen had not been forgotten by society and the

State. The police were intensely concerned with finding him. A lot of people were working on his case. A vast and expensive apparatus had been set in motion.

The police didn't have much to go on. But there were circumstances that made it seem probable that there was some sort of connection between Mikael Mogensen's disappearance and Head Clerk Amsted's tragic death.

There were a couple of thick books in Mogensen's little garret room. Books that dealt with explosives and dynamite. Teodor Amsted had also studied those kinds of books during the last days of his life.

There was the gray fabric, pure wool, double-woven Chestertown-Deverill worsted. The material that both the solvent Amsted and the insolvent Mogensen had used for their suits.

There were numerous insignificant details which had not escaped the notice of the police.

There was a pocket watch which had not been pulverized to the extent that might be expected after the terrible explosion.

There was a mysterious letter to Section 14 of the War Ministry, and they wanted to know the identity of its sender.

There was a lottery ticket which had inexplicably vanished from its permanent place in the desk drawer.

There was a sum of money which the ordinarily so impoverished Mogensen had distributed to people at random the last evening he had been seen.

There were a great many things that made it desirable to continue the investigations in secret. The police were not finished with the missing Mogensen and the deceased Amsted.

Bit by bit they gathered evidence. The bits were patiently fitted together like a puzzle that will eventually form a picture.

It took time. It wasn't an ingenious stroke of inspiration of a single detective that came up with the solution. It was the System and the Organization doing its job.

PART TWO

[21]

A MAN IS DRIVING down a country road in his Ford. A pair of hikers is walking in the opposite direction, two young girls with shorts and socks on and nice legs. They give the man in the Ford a friendly wave.

Their waving makes him terribly angry. Maybe a couple of hussies like that think he's flattered because they waved? Do they imagine that he feels honored by it? He's so angry that he takes the time to stop and back up and shout furiously at the girls. "What a couple of dummies! Who asked you to wave?" Maybe they think he can't resist them? "You'd better see about getting home and putting some skirts on! Stupid hussies!" He can't think of anything more to say. So he snarls at them. And his voice cracks.

The girls look at him in surprise. Then they laugh and walk on.

Country and city have met.

The name of the man in the car is Martin Hageholm. He's a restless soul. He's retired and he has inherited money. He should be living in peace and quiet. But he rushes around poking his nose into any number of things and he has a lot of irons in the fire. He has a red face. And when he gets excited, it turns completely blue.

He is indignant about the two girls. He talks out loud to himself and spits. He yanks furiously at the controls of the car, making it tear off down the road in strange jerks.

This is a beautiful part of the country. There is a large lake and meadows and marshes and flat fields. And there are big hills covered with heather and a forest growing on the shifting sands. There are white cliffs and a blue sea.

A little farther inland, where there is clay soil, lie the bigger farms. They are solid, well-kept properties. Their owners are decent people who pay their mortgages and taxes on time. There's only one of them who's having some trouble, in fact. "He ain't gonna be able to make his next payment," says his neighbor. "Heh heh! It's all over for him now. His farm'll have to go on the auction block." His neighbors laugh and rub their hands. "Sure serves him right!" He really doesn't need such a large sum to make his payment, but it's all over for him anyway.

The large landowners associate only with one another. On Sundays they invite each other over for coffee and enormous quantities of pastry. And their wives arrive wearing hats and gloves and eat their slices of buttered French bread with a knife and fork and their little fingers crooked. They're squeamish and scream if a little green worm in the arbor falls down onto the tablecloth on the coffee table: "Ooh!"

But there is one person they can't associate with. It's the "new man." He didn't arrive in these parts until 1901. They can say hello to him and talk with him all right. But they can't invite him to coffee. The new man.

Then there are the smallholders and the smaller landowners. They live on the sand or by the marsh. They work and slave and can just about get by if they work for the large landowners in the winter for two kroner a day and for the vacationers in the summer for a whole lot more. But each of these people is different. There's one who's lazy. And he drinks too. He's even been known to have himself a beer or two on Sundays. What a pig! And there's Anders from the marsh. He's a real down-and-out type who doesn't have any qualms about asking the town for relief. It's a disgrace to have somebody like that living around here.

Then there are the tenant farmers. They lease places that are owned by people who live in Copenhagen. People who don't want the view from their summer houses spoiled. They want a view of the real countryside and the fields during their vacation. It doesn't do any good for a tenant farmer to complain that the rain comes through his thatched roof or that the mud wall is dank and moldy. That's just what makes these crooked old houses so picturesque, after all.

There are a lot of contrasts in this one area. A lot of different kinds of people. A lot of small societies independent of each other. Small, isolated worlds within these same 100 square kilometers.

There is a fishing village where the fishermen rent out houses to people from Copenhagen. They don't like their tenants, who run around with no shirts on and short pants, bathing and sunning themselves as if they weren't quite right in the head. But then that's the way people from the city are. And the villagers do have to make a living from them.

The breakwaters are silted shut. The villagers don't fish anymore. But they've built a seaside hotel, *pensions*, and rest homes. And farther inland there is a historic inn with half-timbered walls and a thatched roof and old lanterns and proverbs on the ceiling beams and imitation leaded-glass windows. "Visit the Historic Inn!" it says on the signs and placards and arrows.

There is a colony of artists who paint the beauties and characteristic features of the region. They are solid, established artists who drive around in cars with their easels and paints, looking for motifs. A domestic servant carries the palette and holds the paintbrushes for the master.

There are skilled craftsmen who are religious fundamentalists and stick to themselves and constitute a little society of their own. They meet in their evangelical chapel to sing and drink an incredible amount of coffee. They are well-to-do people who agree with each other about how much things will cost.

There is also a camp for unemployed young people. It is another independent little world isolated from the outside. The unemployed are here only in the wintertime. People don't want them in the summertime, out of deference to the vacationers. The unemployed men don't have very elegant clothing, and a person might well be frightened by meeting up with a poorly dressed man in the woods.

The farmers aren't too fond of the unemployed either. "Why should they hang around here loafing? Why, they only work a couple of hours a day. And then they get training programs and sports programs to boot. And the state gives them food and lodging, and spending money on top of everything else!"

But there's a lack of manpower on the farms. You offer a farm hand 500 kroner and four days off a year, but it isn't at all certain that he'll accept it. Nope, he'd probably rather goof off and go on relief! Things sure can't go on like this in the long run. Where's the money going to come from?

There are enough problems to occupy people's minds. There are quarrels and antagonisms. Martin Hageholm tears off down the road. He knows all the people in the little houses. He used to be the mailman. He knows everything about everyone else's business and he's never been afraid to pass this knowledge along. People know each other pretty well out here. They aren't always that sorry when things go badly for somebody. Nothing very sensational happens here. But people's minds are kept busy anyway.

One day a stranger came to this part of the country. A mysterious and secretive man. He arrived here in the fall, after the vacationers were long gone.

It was his intention to stay here forever.

He was the object of a great deal of attention and mistrust. Nobody knew anything about him. But they assumed that there had to be something fishy about him.

And they were right.

[22]

He arrived on a beautiful, clear fall day.

He arrived on foot from the railroad station. A clean-shaven man wearing glasses and a light raincoat. People turned around and looked at him in the village. He greeted them politely and doffed his hat. But nobody returned his greeting. They just turned to stare at him. People didn't like strangers in these parts. You don't like those you have to make your living from.

He had gone into the grocer's and bought a box of cheroots. And he had paid for them with a big bill that the grocer wasn't able to change. "Please excuse me. I'm afraid I don't have anything smaller." So the grocer had to go over to the baker's and get it changed. This was obviously a man with a lot of money. He had foreign money in his wallet too.

"My, how everything's changed out here," he said. "But it *has* been almost thirty years since the last time I was here. I've been abroad all that time. In America." Then he had asked where farmer Jens Jensen lived.

"Jens Jensen—well, right straight ahead. Straight down the road. It's out there where the hills start. A long white house with a blue fence. There's a small mailbox on the house."

People stared after him from their houses. "Now who's *that* sashaying along over there?" The well-digger's wife came all the way out of her house and stood on the road gazing after him.

In some of the houses there were dogs that came out and barked. And the man wearing glasses retreated to the other side of the road. "I'll have to buy a walking stick. That'll have to be one of the first things."

The scent of pine needles and fungus and earth drifted out of the woods. Seaweed and salt came from the shore. The scent of ammonia drifted over from the fields where manure had been spread.

On one side of the road there were hills covered with heather, and behind them was the forest. On the other side you could look far out over the countryside with its fields and marshes.

In the heather-covered hills there were small thatch-roofed houses. They looked much more rustic than houses usually look in the country. They were constructed so that they wouldn't offend the eye. They blended in nicely with the landscape. They were especially designed for the hills. There were no gardens or fences. The property was protected only by signs.

On the other side of the road there were a few farms. These were authentic farms with farmers who tilled the soil and complained about the times. There were geraniums and decorative flower pots in the windows and elegant curtains. There were real yards with rock gardens and flagpoles. And there weren't any signs telling you not to walk on the grass.

There's a Ford driving toward the stranger. It's the first vehicle he has met on the road. It slows down, and a man with a red face leans out and peers curiously at this stranger. He has a hunting dog and a rifle in the car with him. His gaze is unwavering and uninhibited. He shouts something, and the stranger turns around nervously.

"Pardon me. What did you say? I didn't hear—"

"It wasn't you. I was talking to the dog!" The man in the car laughs raucously and smacks his dog across the nose. "Can you behave, huh? Can you stay where you're supposed to?" Then he gives the car some gas and drives on.

Jens Jensen's house is easy to find. It has a trim little front yard and a blue fence. And there is a red mailbox on one end of the house. The stranger stands and looks around a little bit. "I wonder if there are any dogs that will jump out when I open the gate?" There isn't a sound to be heard.

Jens Jensen sees the stranger through his window. But he

doesn't come outside. There's no reason why the stranger can't wait a little bit. The stranger opens the gate and latches it considerately behind him. He knocks tentatively at the door. He has to knock several times. Then somebody shouts, "All right, all right! Just come on in!"

"Hello. I presume you must be Mr. Jens Jensen?"

"Yes."

"My name is Johnson—Herbert Johnson. We talked on the telephone."

"Oh, you're the one that wants to rent the apartment. I didn't know you'd be coming so soon. I don't think it's been cleaned up yet."

"I had the impression that I could move in immediately. You said—"

"I couldn't very well know you'd come running out here right away, could I? Don't you have any luggage? Do you want to move in and live here right this minute?"

"Yes, actually, I would like to very much. My suitcases will be arriving later. They're in Copenhagen. I would appreciate it very much if I could move in at once."

"Well, I don't know whether that will be possible just like that, you know. I'll have to talk to my daughter about it. She's the one who has to clean the place up. Karen!... Ka-ren!... Listen, do you think this man can move in right away?"

"Does it have to be right this very minute?"

"Yes, that's what he says."

"Well then I'll have to do a little cleaning up in there."

"I could certainly take a little walk in the meantime. For maybe an hour or so?"

"Yes, that would be a very good idea. It's not so good to be around a place while it's being cleaned up, anyway."

"All right, then I'll say goodbye for now."

"No, listen, wait a minute! I'd kind of like to get the business of the rent taken care of right away. That's the way it's usually done. I'd prefer to have six months' rent in advance. That's the most common thing. And that's what I told you on the phone too. Somebody was just here who wanted to rent the apartment, by the way. But since you were actually first..."

"Of course. Do you want the money right this minute?"

"Yes, it's always kind of nice to have this sort of thing taken care of. That'll be exactly 350 kroner."

"All right. Here you are." The stranger takes out his wallet. Jens Jensen looks at all those big bills. There are some dollars in it too. They just sort of slip out. It looks pleasantly reassuring.

"Thank you. That's fine. Now I'll write you a receipt. Just to do things right. Your name is Johnson, isn't it?"

"Herbert Johnson."

"All right then... Here you are. And I'm sure Karen will have the apartment cleaned up by the time you get back."

[23]

It's so quiet at night. Very soft noises can be heard from a long way off. A motorboat chugging out on the sea. A dog barking miles away.

And it's so dark. So completely and totally dark. When you put the lamp out, not the slightest pale ray of light comes through the small windows.

Mr. Johnson is lying in bed beneath heavy down comforters. They give off an earthy smell. The whole bed smells moldy.

There were problems with the sheets. The sheets weren't included in the rent. Neither were the comforters, for that matter. But there aren't any stores out here where you can buy sheets. So Karen lent him these. She did so without enthusiasm.

The top comforter is extremely hot. But it's stuffed so full that it doesn't cover everything. It doesn't conform to the contours of Mr. Johnson's body. There is always some small part of him that's cold. And when he tries to fix the places where the cold air is slipping through, the comforter generates twice as much heat over the rest of his body. He is bathed in sweat, and some parts of him are freezing.

It's so quiet that he can hear the long-legged wolf spiders scurrying across the wallpaper. There also seems to be a little mouse gnawing away some place. The furniture stands there creaking of its own accord. Something rustles down the wall behind the wallpaper like sand or plaster sliding down. Because it's so quiet that you can hear all these tiny little sounds, the room seems to be full of noise.

If he had had his pocket watch, its ticking would have sounded like a motor. But he doesn't have a watch. He didn't dare keep it.

He struggles with the comforter. He has virtually lost control over his bed. And he thinks about curious things that are no longer any of his concern. He can't decide by himself what he wants to think about. It's just like having a fever.

There's something he had to accomplish. There's something he didn't get done. There's something he absolutely must finish. But he can't concentrate his thoughts on it. There's a red composition book that he has to finish writing in. And there's a yellow composition book. And a blue one. There are a whole lot of compositions he has to finish writing so he can do well in school. There's a German composition and one in English. And his Danish composition. But whatever in the world is he supposed to write about? He has completely forgotten what the subject of the composition was. This is a catastrophe. It is absolutely imperative to write it now. And there's a math assignment. You raise the perpendicular to the hypotenuse. And we know that the sum of the square of the lecterns is equal to . . .

Blithering nonsense! It's this comforter that's got something wrong with it. I'm lying in a bed in a house out here. Jens Jensen is sleeping at the other end of the house. Karen is sleeping too. She has taken off her clothes and is sleeping beneath a comforter too. I wonder what she looks like? I'm sure her body is completely white. She's never gone sunbathing in her life. But she's healthy and strong and has good solid legs. It's too bad she has such a sour look on her face.

If only he knew what time it was. But he doesn't have a watch anymore. His good old watch is gone. It lasted for many years. It had run faithfully ever since his confirmation. It ticked in his vest pocket and on his nightstand. Now it's gone. It couldn't be helped. Circumstances dictated it. Unforeseen circumstances, ha ha.

Why is his heart beating so wildly? Can it be a fever? He ought to take his pulse. But he'd have to have a watch for that too. His heart is pounding and pounding. Maybe it's diseased. Maybe these last few days have been too much. Maybe he'll lie here and die in a terrible house where everything smells of mildew. Die, just when he was going to start living. Start—ha ha—start! There's certainly no question of any fresh start here. My name is Johnson. H. Johnson. I'm not a young man anymore. I've lived a number of years. In America.

There is a long embankment he has to get across. It is infinitely long. He is walking between two bodies of water. Walking from one country to another. It is essential for him to get across it. It is absolutely essential. Somebody is shooting behind him. They're firing cannons inland. Faster! He has to run. It's still so far, so far. But he can't run. An insane fatigue or dullness or weakness has wrapped itself around his legs. He's sinking to his knees. It's almost impossible for him to get up. He has to use all his last, feeble strength. Because he has to get across the embankment. It's essential.

There are sluices under the embankment. Large, strange

sluices with floodgates and locks. The water pours in from one sea to another. It pours in, seething and roaring. It roars and roars...

[24]

A RESTLESS MAN IS DRIVING around in his Ford. He doesn't have anything to do. He's retired. And he has inherited money. But he's busy with any number of things. He has a lot of irons in the fire. He turns up wherever there's something going on.

"So, Jens! Just what kind of critter do you have at your place? Is he from Copenhagen?"

"He's more like one of those American types. He just came back from over there."

"What kind of guy is he?"

"Well, I don't exactly know. But he's got plenty of money. There's no problem there. His whole wallet was full. There was American money too."

"Now what's a guy like that want out here?"

"Well, it's kind of hard to tell. It is sort of funny that he chose to live right here. But he's got to live somewhere, I guess. And I think he was here as a child once. He says he knows this part of the country."

"He hasn't come up here to go hunting, has he?"

"I don't think so. He doesn't have a gun with him, at least. In fact he doesn't have anything with him at all. But I guess it'll be coming later, judging from what he says."

"Yeah, because if that's the case, you can just tell him that he'd better not try shooting on *my* hunting grounds. If he does, he'll have me to deal with. I'll sure fix a guy like that! If he dares to come onto my hunting—"

Hageholm had gotten all worked up. He clenched his fist and got even redder in the face than before.

"I'll tell him," said Jens Jensen calmly. "But I just don't think he's a hunter."

"Just let him try it! I won't take anything from that kind of guy! I'll darn sure fix that big shot if he comes onto my grounds and starts shooting!"

"I'll tell him."

"What does a guy like that want here anyway? Those Copenhageners, they come tearing out here making things expensive for the rest of us for half the year. Are they going to start coming up here in the winter too? God knows what a guy like that's thinking about. I wonder if he really knows what he wants himself."

"It's hard to tell. I can't figure him out."

"Yeah. There are so many weird things going on. People are nuts these days. Did you hear the latest about Anders?"

"Oh, you mean Anders from the marsh? No. What's with him now?"

"Well, now he's gone and written to the Minister of Social Affairs."

"No. He hasn't! He must be out of his mind. Where did you hear that?"

"That's what the mailman said. He showed me the letter himself. It was written clearly enough: To the Minister of Social Affairs."

"Yep, you sure have your connections in the post office. Heh heh."

"But that won't do him any good, will it? Writing to the Minister?"

"He can write to whoever he wants. He won't get on relief in this town. We've taken enough guff from him."

"Yeah, he's nuts, all right."

"I don't know what he is. But he won't get anything as long as I'm on the Parish Council or the Welfare Committee. That's for sure."

"Yeah, you're man enough to handle somebody like that, all right. It's just like the time I was on the Relief Board. The fishermen wanted to collect unemployment. That sounded pretty good, didn't it? But not while I was around!"

"Right, you told me about that before."

"But I said: *No*. And then they complained about it to the Minister. And I got a letter asking how I would 'justify my refusal.'"

"Yes, you told me about that."

"And so I answered: 'I don't know how a fisherman can be "unemployed" as long as the sea is open!'"

"Uh-huh. That was a good one."

"What do you think about that. 'As long as the sea is open' — hee hee hee! That's a good one, ain't it?"

"It sure is... Well, I'd better see about going inside and doing some work."

"Yeah, I've got to get going too. I've got to go take my eel trap down to the river. I've had a big lock made for it. Look here! That'll stand up, all right. And if anyone tries to break it open, then it's *burglary*!"

"Is there somebody who wants to steal your eels, Martin?"

"You never know, with a guy like Anders prowling around the marsh. You just never know. But he'd better watch it. It's burglary if he tries to fool around with my eel trap!"

"You sure know what's what, Martin. You're a good one."

"Yeah. Hee hee hee hee. I can take care of a guy like that! Well, see you later."

And the Ford purrs and starts off. Jens Jensen watches him go. He's a restless soul, that Hageholm.

[25]

Farmer Jens Jensen is a serious man. He's a man people in the parish have confidence in. That's why he holds a number of official positions.

He is a member of the Parish Council. He is a member of the Social Welfare Committee. And he is the local chairman of the National Health Insurance Board. There's nothing irresponsible about him. He doesn't fritter away the resources of the parish. Nobody can lead *him* down the garden path.

An old woman who lives down by Sandet comes to see him. She has rheumatism and other aches and pains, and the doctor hasn't been able to do anything about them. She thought she might go to see the "wise woman" in Gurre or Stenløse. But the doctor says he thinks maybe she'd better try phototherapy and compresses and the like. She can get that at the hospital. And the National Health will pay for it too.

"What's this now?" says Jens Jensen. "Are you going to have phototherapy, Emma? That stuff's pretty expensive."

"Yes, but I think my health insurance should cover it. And the doctor says he thinks so too."

"I see, the two of you think so. I'm not so sure about that. But of course we can always try to *petition* for it. I'll look into it. You can come back again in about a week's time, Emma."

The old woman thanks him and shuffles off again. She isn't very knowledgeable about National Health regulations and she can't know that nobody has to petition for anything. And when she comes back, the local chairman of the Health Insurance Board merely says:

"No, they wouldn't do it. There's nothing that can be done

about it, Emma. They didn't grant it. You'll have to get along without phototherapy. But I'm sure things will be all right."

It's a good thing for the Health Insurance Board to be able to show a nice balance sheet. Jens Jensen himself does not benefit from saving the Board's resources. But then people would rather elect a man to the Parish Council if they know that he understands how to handle other people's money and not just spend it like water. The farmers have confidence in Jens Jensen.

There are so many demands. It's good that there's someone who knows how to show restraint.

People come to Jens Jensen looking for temporary assistance too.

"Do you really want to be a burden on the parish? I wouldn't have believed it of you. Really, aren't you ashamed of yourself?"

"Sure, but there's not supposed to be anything dishonorable about temporary assistance, you know. It shouldn't be considered the same thing as permanent relief."

"Well, relief is relief, no matter how you slice it. So you really aren't ashamed of going on the parish rolls? It's a good thing your parents aren't around to see this. They'd sink into the ground from shame."

Jens Jensen convinces a lot of people to give up their dishonorable intentions. But there are troublemakers too. Stubborn people who study the law and know it better than the authorities do. And perhaps they'll write to the county complaining that they've been denied relief.

But in that case Jens Jensen has *work* to assign them. Because they're not the sort of people who are afraid of work, are they? Who just don't feel like doing anything because it's more comfortable to collect relief?

"All right, then! Here's work. You can chip rocks. There are plenty of rocks on the beach."

Maybe then those people will realize that it doesn't pay to beat down the doors of the Social Welfare Committee.

Anders from the marsh has been the most persistent. He's a hard one to get rid of. He's stubborn and maybe not quite right in the head.

He was assigned to stone-chipping work. And he did sit on the beach splitting rocks for a while, trying to make a cubic meter per day. But it's no use. And now he comes and hands in his tools saying that he can't take this kind of work.

He simply won't accept the work that is offered to him. But the town doesn't intend to support somebody like that. If the gentleman doesn't want to work, he doesn't have to. But he'd better be a little more careful. Because there's also something called hard labor at the penitentiary.

Jens Jensen's daughter keeps house for Jens Jensen. And she's a good worker.

They don't talk much. They're a quiet family. In the evening Jens Jensen sits with his pipe doing bookkeeping and writing in ledgers. And Karen goes to bed early or sits there without saying anything. If it's peace and quiet the new tenant was looking for out here, there certainly isn't much noise or discord in Jens Jensen's house.

It was different when his wife was alive. Things weren't so quiet then. In those days there was plenty of strife and discord, and people could hear it far and wide.

But then she died, thank God for that. It was definitely the best thing for her. He wasn't good to his wife.

The well-digger's wife can tell strange and horrifying things about Jens Jensen's married life. She was the one who lived the closest and heard most of what was going on.

And if Jens Jensen is so reserved and serious now, it's probably because he doesn't have a completely clear conscience.

[26]

There is frost on the fields in the morning. But the days are clear, and it gets quite warm after the sun has been out for a little while.

Herbert Johnson carefully closes the blue gate behind him when he leaves. He stands a bit and looks out across the marsh. He breathes deeply. He fills himself with the good, invigorating air. It's good for him.

He hasn't told anybody what he did over in America. In any case, you can tell by looking at him that he wasn't a farmer or something like that. It's more likely that he lived surrounded by blotting paper, ink, dust, and filing cabinets.

A rabbit is running along through the marsh. Mr. Johnson watches it until it disappears. But it doesn't need to be afraid of him. He's no hunter. He doesn't shoot things. He doesn't intend to infringe on other people's hunting rights either. Martin Hageholm can rest easy. Herbert Johnson is no poacher. He's not likely to be the cause of any quarrels. He looks so peaceful. If he's a criminal, you sure can't tell by looking at him.

He walks down the country road, vigorously jabbing his new walking stick into the ground. He doesn't meet a soul. There aren't any dogs either. It's a long way between houses out here.

He turns in among the hills on a small, sandy path. There is a magnificent view from up here. On one side is the forest that stretches all the way down to the sea. On the other side the flat country—the marsh, with puddles and peat pits and the river. Behind it there are open fields and plowed land and tiny white houses and farms. And the lake with its strange, dull leaden surface. And behind the lake there are woods and hills.

He's looking out across a map with churches and windmills and extremely small cows. The country road looks like a narrow white stripe down there. He sees a small car driving along the stripe. It's probably Hageholm, the restless soul, out taking a drive.

There are still flowers on some of the heather bushes. Some blue primrose and small yellow sweet everlastings have survived the nighttime frost too. He bends down and picks a couple of the everlastings and sniffs at them. They have a wonderfully aromatic fragrance.

Then all at once he hears an angry voice and he jumps up in fright.

"Hey! You there! What business do you have here? This is private property. What makes you think you can pick my flowers?"

A man in a gray overcoat has suddenly appeared. He is furious, talking in a way he would ordinarily never talk. He is a refined man. He has had the benefit of an excellent upbringing, good schooling, and association with cultivated people.

If he had met Mr. Johnson at a party, he would have been charming and affable. But here on the hills of heather he has forgotten all about European civilization. He is cursing and screaming. He threatens Mr. Johnson with his clenched fist, as if he wanted to start a fight. His proprietary rights have been violated.

"Didn't you see the sign down there? Get moving, will you! What the hell do you think you're doing?"

"You really must excuse me. I really didn't see the sign. And I thought the flowers were wild — that people were free to pick them —"

"Wild! Hell yes, they're wild! But that's no reason to rip them out of the ground! They're *my* flowers! And this is *my* property! And I've sacrificed a pretty penny to put up signs, but people go and take them down. I've laid out over 200 kroner for signs this past year, but they keep disappearing, one right after the other!"

"You must excuse me. I'll go back then. I really didn't see any sign."

"Do you live out here, by any chance?" There almost seems to be a little more mildness in the offended man's voice.

"Yes, I've taken some rooms at Jens Jensen's in the white house down there."

"Oh, I see... Well, in that case it's all right for you to be walking here. People who live out here are certainly welcome to use this path. I've got nothing against that. It's just all those Sunday-Copenhageners I don't want running all over the place. And people had better leave my flowers alone; I absolutely insist on that."

He has become completely friendly now. He has returned to civilization.

"Yes, it is beautiful up here. This is wonderful country. I live up here myself most of the year. In that red house up there!... Dr. Ejegod."

"Johnson."

The two gentlemen greet each other politely.

"And of course you're welcome to walk here as often as you like. I'm just a little sensitive about my flowers. So many dreadful people come out here on Sundays. You understand, I'm sure, that one can get annoyed!"

"Yes, of course. I understand perfectly."

And the two gentlemen tip their hats to each other and go their respective ways.

Dr. Ejegod isn't the only Copenhagener living out here year-round. All of the little farmhouses in the hills are owned by people from Copenhagen. They are cultivated people, well-known people. They are aesthetic people who know how to appreciate nature and make sure that ordinary people don't stray into the panorama. Some of them are artists who paint immortal pictures of the hills and the trees and the summer nights and the will-o'-the-wisp.

Their houses are much more rustic than those of the farmers.

Their thatched roofs have been expressly stipulated by the consortium that sells the lots.

The people who live here aren't vandals or barbarians toward nature. The property owners have dedicated themselves to preserving the hills untouched in their pristine state. Gardens must not be dug. Hedges must not be planted. The heather and the grass and the wild hay are allowed to grow naturally. Denmark's primeval nature lies untouched with its strategically placed Austrian mountain pines and German red spruce and Siberian pines. Nature was voluntarily preserved here before the Society for the Preservation of Nature came into existence.

But the untouched and preserved state is only for the owners. It's only for themselves that they have preserved the hills and the mountain pines. "Private. *Private.* PRIVATE!" Say the signs. And: "*No Trespassing!*" Or: "TRESPASSING PROHIBITED." Not even the roads through the hills may be used by anyone but the property owners. The preservers of nature have reserved only one single, small, neatly laid-out gravel path for chance tourists and Sunday-Copenhageners. People who can only look at nature once a week and who must therefore be presumed to lack the prerequisites to appreciate it. Large signs proclaim that the hills are private property, but "as a special favor on the part of the property owners this path is open to tourists." But walking outside the path is prohibited! "Follow the arrows! To the scenic view!" And between two rows of menacing signs people are herded up to a bench at an observation point from which, as a special favor from the property owners, they are permitted to gaze out across the world free of charge.

Herbert Johnson has reached the gravel tourist path. Now he follows it back to the road. He walks along the fine gravel feeling somewhat dispirited. He no longer stops to gaze around and fill his lungs with air to experience nature. He has a strangely oppressive feeling in his chest.

Herbert Johnson is a decent man. And a law-abiding man. At

least it's his innermost nature to be law-abiding. No matter what might have happened to him and no matter what circumstances might have led him to do.

He walks obediently on the gravel and makes sure not to trample the heather and the wild hay.

[27]

There's been a change in the weather. It's been raining so much the water is standing in pools outside the blue fence. The wind is howling fiercely in the chimney and the telephone poles. It's no weather to be vacationing in the country.

Herbert Johnson wanders around aimlessly in his two small, low-ceilinged rooms. They are very dark. The wallpaper is brown and drab. Not something with flowers and arabesques that are entertaining to look at and contemplate when you're lying in bed in the morning. It's "Moderne Wallpaper" with Chinese rectangles from the Co-op.

There is a brass hanging lamp in the middle of the living room. And in spite of the season there are flies on its brass ornamentation and glass dangles. There is an overstuffed sofa, and there are some easy chairs with very bad springs beneath their upholstery. And there are pictures on the walls of the Jensen family taken on special occasions. The late Mrs. Jensen has been enlarged and retouched and is smiling as if there had never been anything wrong. Jens Jensen as a soldier is set in a fretwork frame.

There is a green porcelain centerpiece on the oval table. In the centerpiece are two ceramic apples.

In the small kitchen there is a primus stove which he bought himself. But he's scared to death every time he has to light it. It's a dangerous apparatus. Technical things are not Mr. Johnson's specialty. It can't have been technology he worked with in America.

He makes his tea himself in the morning and evening. He also has a tin box with bread in it and a crock of butter and a piece of shepherd's cheese wrapped in paper. Karen comes in and makes his dinner. She receives extra payment for this. She cleans his rooms too.

But there are so many problems in daily life that he didn't foresee. He's not a practical man.

There's a problem with his socks, which have gotten holes in them. There's a problem with his collars, which have gotten dirty. There's a problem with his shirts, which nobody lays out for him.

When he was a child, it was his mother who laid out his socks and his clean shirt for him. Later, after he had received his university degree, it was his wife. "All right, I've put your shirt there on the bed. Put it on now." It's been a habit for 46 years. It wasn't independence that he learned in school or at the university. And even though he was in America, he certainly didn't become a practical man.

He's never shined a pair of shoes. He's never made a bed. He's never fried an egg. His mother saw to it that he had a clean handkerchief to take to school every day. And his wife would call out after him as he left for the office, "Did you remember your handkerchief?"

But now all his handkerchiefs are so black and filthy he is disgusted with himself. Where do you get something like that washed out here? There aren't any laundries. And even if there were, how would you go about it? How do you get all the laundry in the right piles? These are problems he hasn't faced before.

He's cold. The storm is wailing in his woodstove, which has a bellowing stag on its door. But there isn't any firewood or any coke briquettes. Where do you get that sort of thing?

You can buy firewood in the forest by the cubic meter, Jens Jensen tells him. But it has to be cut and split. Who's going to do that? Jens Jensen himself has an enormous pile of firewood in his yard. So even if Herbert Johnson did manage to buy some firewood in the forest, and hired a man to saw it and split it and stack it up, where would he put his stack? He doesn't have any space, after all. And when Jens Jensen is questioned about this, he answers sullenly that he doesn't know and it's none of his concern.

Jens Jensen isn't a friendly man. He is serious and somber and has plenty to think about.

But of course you can always buy firewood from the grocer in the village. And the sawmill sells firewood too. Jens Jensen doesn't understand all this helplessness.

But it isn't so easy to adapt to things when you're not used to it. It isn't easy to arrange your own life when other people have always done it for you.

When you've gone to school for twelve years where there were teachers who told you what to do and what to learn and what to know and what to think. When you've never been able to choose but have been made to do what had to be done.

And school doesn't end just because you pass your final exams. There are other exams after that. You're made to study and listen and repeat. Studying consists of learning things by heart. Knowledge consists of repeating opinions. And when the last exam is over, you move into an office—perhaps in a ministry where what you're supposed to do and say and write is also decided for you.

It isn't easy to be independent when other people have made all the decisions for you for 46 years.

He's been a schoolboy for far too long. Almost all his life. He has learned duty and discipline and order and punctiliousness.

He has been under the guardianship of his parents and teachers and wife and Section Chief. He has been primed and brought up and bent and molded and prepared for something that other people wanted. His whole life has been a preparation for something else. When he was born, the most important problem was whether he would be able to draw a pension when he was 65. It was never *now*. It was always for *later*. There has been far too much school.

He knows that *utor* and *fruor* and *fungor* and *potior* as well as *vescor* govern the object in the ablative, and that *quis* is to be preferred to *aliquis* after *si* and *nisi*, *ne*, and *num*. And he also knows something about the sine and cosine of opposite and adjacent angles. And he knows many, many legal paragraphs and statistics. It wasn't out of a thirst for knowledge that he acquired all this information. He wasn't curious about sine relationships or the Battle of Pavia (1525) or the law of contracts and torts. It wasn't from any desire for knowledge that he studied these things. It was merely because it was assigned as homework. It was necessary in order for him to go farther. It was his duty, his course syllabus, his preparation so that he would be able to draw a pension.

Herbert Johnson is walking back and forth in his small rooms. He looks out at the rain and feels slightly cold.

Why is he here? What does he intend to do? He came out here of his own free will. For the first time in his life he made a decision on his own.

There were several circumstances that made him do it. He's no revolutionary. There is nothing reckless about him. But deep, deep inside him there must have been a tiny scrap of a will to live. A small desire to have control over his own life, some yearning for freedom.

It was a mere coincidence that his desire happened to come to fruition. And now he is involved in something whose outcome he cannot predict. Now one thing is leading to another.

And now he's stuck out here. Mr. H. Johnson from America.

[28]

It's November. This is the month when the inhabitants of Denmark are counted. A census and an official count of the population are taken. For other people this is only a small matter, but Mr. Herbert Johnson from America starts in fright when Jens Jensen brings him a census form and asks him to fill it out accurately and legibly. This is a new problem, which makes his heart pound violently.

He has to ask to be allowed to borrow a pen and a bottle of ink. He doesn't own anything like that himself. He never writes letters. And his hand shakes when he goes to fill in the blanks, making his handwriting look distorted and unnatural.

He thinks for a long time before he can recall his birthday. Is he married, unmarried, or a widower? It takes him a long time to decide. How many children? None, of course.

Number, letter, and classification in the military draft records? It will probably be sufficient to write down that he was rejected for military service. Domicile during November of last year? "Nebraska!"

This sort of thing is easy enough for other people, but Herbert Johnson has turned completely pale and can hardly get his breath. And now it's essential to remember what he has written. For future reference. Maybe he really ought to make a copy.

He is nervous, shattered, sick. It's as if the schoolboy of 46 is cheating on a composition for the first time or changing his report card. He has never tried this before. He's too late. He waited too long with everything. If you're going to play hooky from school, you shouldn't wait until you're 46.

"Year and date of birth? (Write legibly!)"

Year of birth... 46 years old. Well then, he's an adult, after all! Actually, it hasn't been all that long since he was in school.

In the old gray building on Frue Plads. One of the teachers would be lying in wait for those who were late. In the morning they would sing devotions. "The blessed day with joy we behold." They stood pressed tightly together in an assembly room. It smelled of wet clothes and sandwich paper and oiled leather boots. And they were afraid of first period, with a raging mathematics teacher. And of third period, with a sadistic French teacher.

He ran the whole way to school in order not to be late. And when it was spring, and the bushes were green in Kongens Have, and when the lawns were fragrant, and when there were starlings singing, and trees blossoming, he could very easily feel a faint temptation to stay away from school. And while he was running in order not to be late, he would think of fields and grain and forests. And about people who do what they feel like and choose the direction they want to walk. But he never stopped. He ran straight into the jaws of the school. He felt the urge to play hooky. But he never did.

He has never played hooky until now. But isn't it too late to be playing hooky from school when you're 46 years old?

"Year and date of birth? Occupation?"

Now why do these people have to know his occupation too? He has come home from America to live in this part of the country. And he intends to live on the money he made over there. So, he's independently wealthy.

Occupation: "Independently wealthy."

"Married, unmarried, or widower?"

There's no doubt here. He's *unmarried*, of course. He has never even been in love. He once had this thing about a kiosk lady, when he was in high school. But that was only a silly childish crush. No. He isn't married. Perhaps he vaguely remembers a woman who essentially replaced his mother and who administered him and an apartment and a household. She laid out his underwear for him and she went through his pockets and cleaned the pocket lint out of them and gave the maid instructions about his breakfast: One soft-boiled egg and two pieces of white bread and *one* piece of rye bread. He *never* eats anything else. "Here's your briefcase, and here's a clean handkerchief! Just don't forget it. You'd better go now, or else you'll be late for work... Your dinner's ready now. You'd better come now, or else it'll get cold. Here's one more piece. Now eat!"

"*Unmarried.*"

"Number of children under fifteen?"

"*None.*" He has no children. When you're unmarried, you don't have any children either. He cleans his glasses. He spends a long time polishing them with a dirty handkerchief. He isn't used to wearing glasses. And these glasses he has aren't much good anyway. They have ordinary window glass in them. But he looks totally different when he has them on. Nobody would recognize him.

He reads through the form. Then he waves it in the air so it will dry. For his entire life he has lived surrounded by blotting paper and blotting pads. But now he doesn't own a single one.

There is a large envelope for the form. He folds up the form and stuffs it in the envelope and carefully seals it shut. Can he possibly imagine that he can conceal his circumstances from Jens Jensen? He has forgotten that Jens Jensen is one of the authorities. That he is a member of the Parish Council and is partially responsible for the proper completion of census forms.

Mr. Johnson walks out through the little blue gate and delivers the big envelope next door. "Here you are. I think everything is in order."

[29]

SHOTS RING OUT down in the marsh. And shots ring out in the forest. All the hunters in the area are out shooting. The important thing now is to make sure that nobody enters your hunting grounds unlawfully. The locals are busy reporting each other for illegal hunting.

The bicycle mechanic is walking along with his gun and his little old dog. And Hageholm, wearing a hunting outfit with a feather in his hat and a hunting bag and binoculars, is driving along in his Ford. And when he sees the bicycle mechanic, he stops and rolls down his window and screams shrilly across the road, "If I meet up with you on my hunting grounds, you'll get yourself a good thrashing!"

And the bicycle mechanic makes an angry, threatening gesture at him and yells, "If I see you on mine, you'll be shot on the spot! Now you've been warned!"

Then Hageholm drives on. And the bicycle mechanic swaggers off with his rifle and his old dog.

Hageholm is a good hunter. He has money and has leased the best hunting preserve out here. He brings a lot of rabbits home in his car. And sometimes a deer too. Of course eating all this game is out of the question. And a true hunter doesn't shoot game in order to sell it. On the other hand, Hageholm doesn't like to give anything away. The numerous rabbits and deer are cleaned, dressed, carved up, roasted, and preserved in mason jars. In the autumn Johanne is busy boiling game and preserving rabbits. She has been his housekeeper for over forty years—ever since the time his wife was still alive. They sleep together in the white-enameled double bed, but the people in these parts don't quite know whether they're just keeping each other warm or leading a filthy and indecent life. On a piece of embroidery over the bed it says, "JESUS LIVES."

When Hageholm retired from the post office, he bought a house—or rather a *villa,* as he calls it. It's a nice, new house made of gray concrete with a red roof and red stripes on it. Hageholm put a lot of money into it. He had a rectangular pillar cast with a ball on top for each side of the driveway. He had a flagpole with a gilded glass finial erected in the middle of the circular lawn in front of the house. In the summer he rents out the second floor to people from Copenhagen; then his mortgage and interest are paid for the entire year.

He is industrious and full of energy. He keeps rabbits in his yard and bees in the garden behind his house. His chicken coop is a model structure that is admired by his neighbors. He has hunting dogs that he rules over. And he rules over fat old Johanne and orders her around as if she were an entire regiment of recruits. He was a sergeant at one time. Then he became a police officer. And when he was dismissed from the police force, he became a rural mailman.

They talk a great deal out here about his brief stint as a rural police officer. He certainly wasn't dismissed on account of his virtues. He was probably a little too eager about his duties. A little too zealous. But the worst of it is that he still seems to think of himself as some sort of policeman.

They also say that he read people's letters when he was a mailman. He would hand over a letter or the county newspaper with great dignity. And he was Santa Claus incarnate when, on rare occasions, he would bring a money order or a registered letter containing cash. But when he arrived with payment notices, he acted like the offended creditor himself. "See to it that this is paid!" he would say harshly. "This notice will be held at the post office for three days. You'll have to get it taken care of before then!"

His occupation gave him an intimate knowledge about people's circumstances. And he felt himself justified in prying into a lot of things that could not be considered any of his business. He wasn't really popular. "He's a little too busy with other people's affairs," they said. "He'd do better to mind his own business. He wasn't too good to his wife when she was alive. It's probably wisest not to talk about it too much. Or about the way he inherited his money either. No, he'd do better to mind his own business instead."

He has a hard time being retired. He bought himself a car so he can drive his old route several times a day. He takes care of his rabbits, dogs, bees, and his hunting grounds and eel traps. And he has countless quarrels and lawsuits going on with people. That's something that needs taking care of too.

He is gathering provisions as if the village were facing an impending siege or a famine. Firewood is heaped up in huge piles in his yard. It is stacked up meticulously and artfully with a sloping roof over it and gutters for the rain. He has firewood here for years to come, and new wood is constantly added every time an opportunity to get it cheaply presents itself.

He can confront harsh winters and famine with peace of mind. His cellars are full of provisions. He has herbs and roots in boxes of sand. He has juice and preserves on shelves. The oldest of the jars are ten years old. But every fall Johanne puts up more so that the surplus increases. He has large and small pickled cucumbers and pickled vegetables and pickled beets that have to be re-boiled every year so they will keep. He has peas and beans and carrots and cauliflower and asparagus in mason jars. And he has preserved rabbits and deer and birds. He has jars of pork chops and jars of roast chickens. His poultry yard is swarming with live chickens, but every so often he slaughters and roasts them and puts them into hermetically sealed jars. He hasn't tasted fresh food in many years. When he and Johanne eat chicken, it's always from the year before last.

He has a weird and unquenchable mania for collecting things.

His cellar resembles a museum with anatomical specimens preserved in alcohol. He takes all his guests down there to show them his collection; they shudder in amazement.

"Yep, Johanne is real good at canning things," says Hageholm. "She's a real jewel." He nudges her in the side so she twitches her mouth and tells him to behave decently.

He strides around in his cellar looking at his specimens like the curator of a museum. "These jellied apples are certainly keeping well. Those pig's knuckles still look good. That was the pig we slaughtered when my daughter was still alive. Ah yes, it's good to have something in the house."

The jars that have gotten a little moldy on top are set aside for re-preserving. Johanne takes care of them.

Hageholm strolls around contemplating his singular collection with affection and tenderness. And fat Johanne with her tiny little eyes flitting back and forth is like an attendant guarding the museum's treasures.

"We'll have to get a few more blackberries preserved this year," she says. "And some plums before we get a frost."

They're a strange couple with strange interests. God only knows what their life together is really like.

[30]

"You really ought to come over and live at my place, you know. It's a much better apartment than Jens Jensen's. It's got electric lights and everything. It wouldn't be much more expensive for you. And it's far more *centrally* located!"

Hageholm and Johnson have been having a chat on the country road. Johnson is out taking a walk with his walking stick and his collar turned up around his ears. It's raining slightly, and the wind is blowing. It's cold to be standing there talking.

"How much is it you're paying at Jensen's place?"

"700 a year."

"700... hmm, so that's what he gets. Well, that's far too much for that hole. Why, it's cramped and damp and doesn't have any modern conveniences. You could live at my place for 1000. That's what I take in for the summer alone. But if the tenant is quiet and easy to get along with and will be living there permanently and is somebody you can depend on, well then he could live there the entire year for that amount. It's cheap, I'll tell you. It's close to the grocer's and the station and everything. And it's got electric lights and a telephone you could borrow if need be."

"Yes, but now I'm living at Jens Jensen's place, you see. A person can't just move out early. And I'm actually pretty happy with it."

"Hmm, no, of course not. I just mean, if you do make a change sometime. You ought to think it over. Say, wouldn't you like to take a look at my apartment right now, as a matter of fact? Are you busy? Climb into the car. There you go!"

Herbert Johnson is a lonely man. He has nothing against getting better acquainted with the local residents. Besides, Hageholm shouts at him so imperiously, and Johnson is used to doing what people tell him.

"I think you can squeeze in next to that big sack, can't you?"

"Oh yes, thanks, it'll be just fine. What do you have in it?"

"Sugar. There's 200 pounds there. So we won't be running short for the time being, hee hee hee! They said on the radio yesterday that sugar is supposed to start going up now. So it's better to buy things at the right time. We really use quite a bit for canning. And it's something that keeps, after all."

The car swings in between the two concrete pillars with the balls on top and stops in front of the door. Hageholm honks the horn vigorously and shouts, "Johanne! Jo-hanne! Where are you? We've got company!"

Fat Johanne comes out to take a look wearing a white apron. Her little eyes flit about uncertainly as if the stranger knew something about her or could see right through her.

"This is the American from down at Jens Jensen's place!" Hageholm screams from the car.

"Hello," says Herbert Johnson, extending his hand. "This is a beautiful place you have."

Johanne hesitantly puts out her hand. It feels completely dead to the touch. Like a slab of meat.

"Yes, your husband absolutely insisted on bringing me along to show me the apartment..."

Johanne blinks her eyes and twitches her mouth rapidly, but no words come out.

"She's my *housekeeper*," Hageholm says. "My wife is dead... Yes, a person does get lonely. It's been almost thirty years since she died."

"Oh, I see... yes." Herbert Johnson manages to put a sympathetic expression on his face.

"Yes, a person does get lonely," Hageholm sighs. "So it's a good thing I've got her!" He puts his arms around Johanne and pats her behind.

"Oh, now stop it!" she says. "You're awful!"

"Hee hee hee!" says Hageholm. "Yes, sit down, Mr. Johnson, and make yourself at home. Johanne will be here in a minute with a cup of coffee."

"You really mustn't go to any trouble for my sake."

"But we were going to have coffee anyway. It really doesn't make any difference whether we drink it in here or in the kitchen. It's no trouble at all," says Johanne.

She puts a new cloth on the table, and a silver creamer and sugar bowl and sugar tongs. And cookies that she has baked out of flour, water, and margarine.

"These cookies cost almost nothing," says Hageholm. "And they keep so well. Please try them, they taste delicious!"

"Thank you. Oh, yes, they really are delicious."

The late Mrs. Hageholm hangs in enlargement on the wall. She resembles the late Mrs. Jens Jensen. But then it was probably the same photographer who made the enlargements. Another photograph is hanging on the wall too. A young girl with a very broad face.

"That's my daughter," says Hageholm. "Yes, she's dead too. She died here five years ago. There's not much to life when all a person's loved ones have passed away. She had a good position with a wholesaler in Copenhagen. Then she came out here and was going to get married. And then one day she's walking along sucking on a straw—without thinking about it. And then she gets tetanus. And dies. That's the way it can happen. There must have been a *bac-sillus* on the straw. No, 'none knows the day till the sun has set'!... But like our former pastor once said, 'It's strange that it's the best people who must pass away first.' Ah yes, that's the way it is."

"That's very sad," says Herbert Johnson, staring at the photograph on the wall. "So young."

"Yes," says Hageholm. "It's sad to be left alone."

And Johanne dries a tear from her tiny eyes with the edge of her apron.

There are several minutes of gloomy silence. Johnson tries desperately to swallow one of Johanne's cheap, non-perishable cookies. But he doesn't have enough saliva. He needs the help of her weak coffee.

There are also adages hanging on the wall. Bible verses that have been cross-stitched and framed. Hageholm's daughter was probably the one who made that sort of thing. There are deer antlers hanging on the wall and stuffed birds and other hunting trophies. The Bible and hymnal are lying beside the radio. On the windowsill there are flowerpots with red and yellow tulips made of wax.

There is a porcelain boot and other knickknacks on the piano.

"Do you play the piano?" Johnson asks Johanne.

"No, no," she says. "Hageholm's daughter was the one who played."

Johnson has once again touched a painful topic.

"No. And nobody plays it anymore," Hageholm says darkly. "There was a young girl here a while back, and she wanted to play the piano. But I said, 'Stop! *Stop!* It mustn't be touched. The hands that played it are dead now. It must never be touched by another hand!' "

Again there is a moment of solemn silence.

"No," Hageholm finally says. "When my daughter died, I did think about selling the piano. But then they only wanted to give me 25 kroner for it. 'No!' I said then. '*No!* In that case it will stay here!' "

"Yes, it was a good thing you didn't sell it at that price," says Johanne. And Hageholm repeats, as if he were reciting it, that the hands that played the piano are dead now. And no human hand shall touch it as long as he lives. What happens after he is no more is for others to decide. He glowers at Johnson as if he suspects him of wanting to start playing his daughter's piano.

This is a Christian house. There are adages on the walls. And there is a Bible and a hymnal. And Hageholm never curses, as hot-tempered as he normally is. But he makes up for it by the extensive use of crude vulgarities. While Johanne is clearing the table, he begins—for no apparent reason—a story about Frederik VII and a peasant with a stomachache. He laughs uproariously, and Johnson politely laughs along with him.

Herbert Johnson had been prepared to have Hageholm interrogate him about America and other matters. But he can set his mind at ease. Hageholm does all the talking himself. One incomprehensible story after another. And of course he includes the off-color stories from his army days too. There's no end to them.

Johnson would like to look at his watch. But of course he doesn't have any watch to look at.

"Hmm—I'm sure it's getting rather late. I'll have to see about getting back home."

"Yes, but there was the apartment you were supposed to look at. Johanne! Come along and show the American the apartment!"

[31]

Mr. Johnson has nothing but compliments and praise for Hageholm's apartment. But the thing is, now he's living at Jens Jensen's place and has agreed to stay there a year. "But after that... perhaps..."

"Of course," says Hageholm. "As you wish. But I just want to tell you that you shouldn't trust Jens Jensen too far. He can be a little underhanded. That's not the sort of man for you." Hageholm doesn't want to say anything bad about him, but it's always a good thing to be forewarned.

Hageholm shows him the rest of the house too. And the provisions in the cellar, the poultry, and the firewood.

"Well, you certainly do have a nice place," says Herbert Johnson.

"Yes, it's nice. It sure is. But what good is it all? I'm a lonely man. The people I was supposed to share it with are lying in the cemetery now."

Mr. Johnson mumbles his condolences.

They're sitting in the living room, and Hageholm offers him a cigar, a very special and extraordinary occurrence. And they drink a glass of Hageholm's homemade wine that tastes like Vaseline. Fat Johanne has retired to the kitchen.

They look up at the enlarged photograph of Mrs. Hageholm

in the gilded oval frame. "Yes, she was pretty once," Hageholm says. "But of course it didn't last. She wasn't a *natural* woman. No, she wasn't." And Hageholm leans forward toward his guest and says meaningfully, "When women don't want to have children, then there's something wrong with them! It's unnatural for a woman not to have children."

Hageholm sighs heavily. It's not often that he has a chance to open his heart. He has suddenly become quite familiar with this stranger from America. He tells him about his marriage and his tribulations, and how he came to inherit the money that he bought the house and everything else with. "Because an ordinary post-office pension wouldn't have covered all this, you know."

It was his wife's family who were well-to-do, you see. Her father was a large landowner in these parts and he had 100,000 kroner. She was a damn good catch. But her father didn't like the rural mailman. He tried to discourage him in every way possible and did everything to prevent the two young people from getting married. And he made a will stipulating that neither his daughter nor Hageholm, but only their children, could inherit his money.

He did that because he knew that his daughter had a disease of the womb and wasn't strong enough to have children. "No, she wasn't a natural woman."

But Hageholm wasn't a man to give up that easily. No sir, he went to it with his wife and put her in the family way. But it was an awful delivery. And it was back when they didn't have cars and things like that. The doctor came from far away in a buggy. Back then they lived all the way down in the fishing village. It was before the railroad too. It was lonely out here back then. "Oh boy, oh boy — it was pretty bad. They destroyed the baby, cut it all to pieces."

So of course there was nothing else to do but try again, even though his wife didn't want to. Because she wasn't a natural woman, and she was afraid. "When it gets so that women don't want to have babies, where are we then?"

But the second time it did go better. This time it was a daughter, who survived, and who would eventually inherit her grandfather's money. But after that delivery his wife died. She had her good points, of course, there's no denying that. But she *was* kind of sickly. Hysterical and things like that. She wasn't a *natural* woman.

And then his daughter died of tetanus. It was right before she was going to get married. So Hageholm got the darn money after all! If the old man had only known that. Hee hee hee! And Hageholm pokes Mr. Johnson in the side.

But then he remembers his grief and sighs deeply. And as far as the piano is concerned, no hand shall touch it again! Because the hands that played it are dead now...

[32]

HERBERT JOHNSON ARRIVED with no baggage. But there are many things he can't do without and that you can't get at the local grocery store: overshoes, an umbrella, and warm sweaters. He's never lived in the country in the winter before and didn't know how cold it could be.

It will be necessary for him to take a trip to the nearest big town. It's not far, and Herbert Johnson has been there before. He stopped off there on his way here. Among other things he was in a barber shop to have his little mustache removed.

That wasn't wise or well thought out. If you want to get rid of your mustache, perhaps because you wish to alter your appearance for one reason or another, you shouldn't have it done in a small town where a peculiar person and an unusual customer will be remembered. This wound up hurting him later on.

Now Mr. Johnson is on his way back to this town to do some shopping.

There is a little railroad line between the fishing village and the town. The little electrified train purrs off through the countryside and through the big forest. In the summertime it's a real train with a lot of cars. But in the wintertime it's a single electric car. An odd, short little car.

The passengers know the engineer, and people say hello to each other when they get on and ask the others if they're taking a trip. There is a woman with a little boy, and the boy has to heed the call of nature. "Isn't there a toilet on this train?" the woman asks.

"No, not in this car. But we can certainly stop here," the engineer says, slowing down. "Or maybe it's too open here? Then we'll drive on to that bush over there." And the woman gets off and holds the little boy in front of her. Then they climb back into the car, and the express rolls on.

It's a quaint little railroad line. It was even quainter when it was steam-powered, and they fired the tiny locomotives with peat. But it goes faster now, and that's very nice. The engineer misses the locomotives. "Things were still better back then," he says. "Locomotives are really a lot different from one of these electric cars."

"Why are they better?"

"Well, you know. A locomotive's a *locomotive* after all!" And there really isn't any arguing with that.

And then there's the bus. You can also take the bus when you're going to town. And perhaps it is the best means of transportation. It drives right through the middle of the villages and stops outside peoples' houses. Everybody knows everybody else here. "Hi there, Emma! Are you going over to your children's again?" the bus driver asks. "Oh, hi there, Niels! How are things going with the Parish Council?"

A man is standing and waving to stop the bus. "Say, Harald," he says to the bus driver. "Could you just take this marble plaque with you? All you have to do is lift it over the cemetery wall across from the grocer's."

"Sure, I think I can do that." The plaque is put on board, and the bus stops at the cemetery, and Harald manages to get the grave marker over the wall and carefully stand it upright.

On Thursdays and Sundays especially there are a lot of people on the bus. These are people who are going to see the wise woman. She receives people every day, of course, but Thursdays and Sundays are actually supposed to be best. The *constellations* are best on those days. There's supposed to be a little mystique about it, after all. But apart from that the wise woman is all right. She's best at curing rheumatism and sciatica and neuralgia and aches and pains in the joints. All these skeptical people, who are usually so suspicious, have faith in her. These doctors are supposed to be so darn smart, but people still have more faith in the woman and her ointments.

It's not the dimwits who seek her out. It's the enlightened men of the area. Members of the Parish Council and people who know what's what. Jens Jensen goes to see the wise woman too, whenever he has something wrong with him. And he's even the local chairman of the National Health Insurance Board.

They talk politics on the bus. "Things can't keep on like this! Things are going to hell. Where's the money going to come from? They think you can just keep subsidizing and subsidizing. But after you get people out of the habit of doing anything, you're in real trouble! And it's almost impossible to get a farm-hand anymore!" the large landowners say. "Who can afford to pay the wages they're supposed to get now? And they're supposed to get a vacation too! What are things coming to? Was there any such thing as a vacation in our day?"

The bus driver gets involved in the discussion and says he thinks that vacations are a good thing. And they really shouldn't complain so much. People are worse off other places in the world.

They also talk global politics in the bus. "Those Japanese sure are asking for it!" the bus driver says. "And the big powers just stand there watching. So what do people think about it in America?" The American from Jens Jensen's place is questioned about the political situation. But he can only agree with the others, that it doesn't look good. He doesn't read the newspapers and he doesn't know what has been happening in the world.

The American was supposed to have done his shopping in town. But then it occurs to him that he might just as well go all the way into Copenhagen. He has plenty of time, and isn't missing anything. Still, it's a foolish idea on his part. Other people can go wherever they want. But he'd be better off keeping to himself and not exposing himself to any risks.

But he does some rash and dangerous things in Copenhagen too. It's only by chance that things go well for him. He could just as easily have gotten mixed up in catastrophic difficulties. And all merely for the sake of a foolish idea. Because of a sudden impulse.

This man, who leads a quiet, unobtrusive life in the country, suddenly feels an irresistible urge to go out to Assistens Cemetery. This is one place where he definitely should not show his face.

[33]

A THAW HAS SET IN, and snow has fallen. It's wet and slippery on Nørrebrogade and Kapelvej. But inside Assistens Cemetery there is still some snow on the ground.

The solitary man walking around looking for something leaves big wet footprints in the snow with his overshoes. He has a fur hat pulled down over his ears, and the collar of his coat is turned up so you can barely see his face. He has large glasses on and he is leaning on a rustic oak walking stick.

He peers around in a strangely probing, cautious manner. The cemetery attendant has noticed him and watches him somewhat suspiciously. "Now I wonder what sort of a person he is? It isn't somebody who wants to steal flowers, is it?" There aren't many flowers on the graves this time of year, but the ones that are there are expensive.

He slowly follows the strange visitor.

The man in the fur hat looks back. He doesn't like policemen and attendants and people like that. He walks faster in order to get out of sight, but the attendant walks a little faster too.

The man turns down small side paths. He is wandering around among the graves in a totally aimless manner. It's as if he's walking in a labyrinth and can't find his way out again. His overshoes leave their big wet tracks on all the small white paths.

"Hello there, are you looking for something? Can I help you?"

He jumps at the sound of the attendant's voice. "Uh, no thank you . . . well, yes — that is, I'm looking for a grave. A man I knew. A colleague of mine. I know he's supposed to be buried in this cemetery, but I can't find the spot. His name was Amsted. He committed suicide."

"Oh yes, the one who blew himself up. He's over there in the new section. I can take you over to it if you'd like."

Things look rather desolate in the new section. Many of the graves are completely covered with withered wreaths. They haven't been fixed up yet. The earth has to settle a little bit first, if the graves weren't packed down.

"It's over there. The one with the new stone."

"Thank you very much."

"Don't mention it, sir." The attendant tips his cap and withdraws. This certainly isn't any graverobber. There is no danger to the small tulips lying on the snow beside several of the graves.

Herbert Johnson stares at the gravestone. It is an unhewn stone. Simple and beautiful. *Teodor Amsted*, it says on it. And underneath, the word: PEACE.

Now why should it say *Peace*, of all things? Why did she come up with that?

A thick layer of fir branches has been placed on the grave. The twigs of fir poke out through the melting snow. Outside the cemetery walls he can hear streetcars and automobiles and bicycle bells. But in here there is not a single person.

He suddenly feels the cold in spite of his overcoat and overshoes and fur hat. It's so absurdly gloomy here. It's a strange sensation to be standing beside your own grave. It gives you a feeling of great loneliness. PEACE, it says. PEACE.

Here stands Teodor Amsted criticizing his wife's arrangements. He has never criticized her before. But this PEACE annoys him no end.

He stands there figuring things up. It's only been about two months since he was buried. And there's already a stone on his grave. And they've spread out fir branches and everything. It makes him think about the account of a funeral he read in the newspaper. It was so strange: "He went away like unto the setting of the harvest sun." Why had the reporter quoted that specific line from the hymn? And why did they write PEACE on the stone, of all things?

He wasn't a critical man when he was alive. But after his death he is dissatisfied with everything all of a sudden. PEACE — simple and beautiful. He knows how she would say it. He can almost hear her voice.

He looks around in fright. She might show up here, after all. She might just get the idea of putting some little tulips with greenery and holly on his grave. On *Mikael Mogensen's grave*. That strange Mikael Mogensen to whom he gave his discarded suits. His friend and classmate from school. He was such a good student. They were both among the best students in the class. They were sure to make something out of themselves, people said. But being among the best students in the class doesn't seem to mean so much somehow. Here he is standing beside his own grave like a ghost. He feels like throwing up. It makes him think about a disgusting sight out on the Common. "*Teodor Amsted*. PEACE."

It was supposed to have been the beginning of a whole new life. But now he can't tear himself away from a grave and a gravestone. His own grave. His school classmate's grave.

It's starting to get dark. Then a bell begins to ring, frantically and noisily. It's ringing so people will leave. The cemetery is going to close.

He is running. He leaves new black footprints in the snow on the walkways. He is running toward the exit as if he were pursued by ghosts.

The brightly lit streetcars are clanging their bells on Nørrebrogade. It's snowing again. It's snowing in the shop windows too, with cotton snow. They are decorated for Christmas with elves and other things. The casket store is decorated for Christmas too. There aren't any elves in the window, but there are fir branches around the coffins that stand there open and inviting, all ready to lie right down in.

The snow is falling in big wet blobs. The asphalt is slippery and wet. There's a man selling Christmas trees on a corner. Somebody's collecting money for the Salvation Army: "Keep the pot boiling!" Children are selling little jumping jacks on strings and paper roses.

Everything is all so peculiar. It's so strangely irrelevant to him. There are a lot of people on the street. But he has nothing to do with them. He's outside of it all. He's a ghost from the cemetery.

It's so cold. He can feel that he's starting to catch a cold. He buys some little black throat lozenges in a candy store. He almost seems to be doing it in his sleep. This must be what being drunk is like.

He catches the train at Nørreport Station. It's warm and bright and homey in the train. It's almost like coming back to life again. Just like waking up after you've been dreaming.

Only now does he notice that he's hungry, and that he hasn't eaten anything all day. He has a couple of cheroots in his pocket. And here are his matches.

He leans back comfortably in his seat and puffs away. Herbert Johnson is coming back. He's been on a trip to the city. It was a stupid and senseless journey. But now he's coming back.

[34]

OUT IN THE COUNTRY the snow is sticking. It's perfect Christmas weather.

The woods are strangely changed. Herbert Johnson is taking a walk with his walking stick and overshoes. He's the first person to step on the new snow. Otherwise there are only animal tracks. You can see where the rabbits have been hopping like kangaroos, and you can see where the fox has been dragging its tail along behind him, leaving a streak in the snow.

If you're lucky, you might just see the fox himself. His fur is a pretty red color now, as he stands peering at the solitary man.

Straight fire lanes pass through the woods all the way down to the shore. Other lanes cut across them. From a hill you can look far down one of these cross lanes. It must be miles long. Lord knows where it ends. Someday he should keep following it and see where he ends up. Maybe this coming spring when the days grow longer...

Closer to the shore the trees get smaller. Until finally they're lying on the ground twisting and coiling around themselves. But they stay alive and hang on despite the sand and the salt and the wind.

The beach looks strange with the snow on the dunes and the snow on the white sand. You can't tell the difference between the snow and the sea foam.

Large seagulls are hovering around over the beach. Otherwise it's totally deserted.

Some boats are tied up over at the fishing village. There is snow on the anchors and buoys and fishing gear. The bathing huts stand there empty and cold.

Behind them is the large public parking lot. But there are no cars there now. Some men are sitting there crushing rocks. They've made big piles of chips that aren't going to be used for anything. These are men who were assigned work by the town. People who have applied for Jens Jensen's relief fund. You can't just get money for nothing.

Every so often Jens Jensen bicycles down here himself to see how things are going. It's not pleasant sitting here, but it's not supposed to be either. The town doesn't have any use for the chips, but someday it might. It gives the unemployed something to do.

It's only that cantankerous Anders from the marsh who has refused to split rocks. He can't take this work, he says. He's crooked and bent over with rheumatism and has to walk several kilometers to get down here.

That's his problem, says Jens Jensen. If he can afford not to accept the work assigned to him, then he can do without.

Herbert Johnson has talked with Anders several times. He's harmless enough, actually, but a little strange and eccentric. He has a wife and three nice children, and he's good about playing with his children and making little ships and windmills for them. But you can't make a living doing that. Maybe you can't by chipping stones either. It's piecework, and when you're half starving and sickly, you can't earn much by it. But he didn't need to be half starving. Jens Jensen once had the baker send him two large loaves of rye bread at the town's expense. But maybe Anders is used to something better. Maybe he'd rather have roast goose. He's a troublemaker, and Jens Jensen and the town have put up with a lot from him. But there'll have to be an end to it someday.

Herbert Johnson has a number of possibilities for varying his solitary walks. There's the woods, the beach, the marsh, and the road. He can walk to the station and watch the train come in. And he can walk down to the ruin too; it is romantically overgrown with vegetation, and in front of it there's a white gate and a flagpole and benches and wastebaskets and regulations.

Or he can walk down to the inn (the "historic" one) and drink coffee. There's no one who knows the history of the inn. But it has imitation leading painted on its windows, and its façade has been painted to look half-timbered and decorated with old proverbs. Inside there is a beamed ceiling, a cozy atmosphere, and an open fireplace with red bricks in a Flemish pattern painted on its cement.

He likes the cozy atmosphere. There's an attractive girl behind the counter who gives him a friendly smile and asks where he's from and talks about the weather. She is much friendlier than Jens Jensen's Karen.

Herbert Johnson would come here much more often if it weren't for the "witty man." The "witty man" lives at the inn free of charge in exchange for entertaining the guests. As soon as an unsuspecting stranger walks in, the "witty man" rushes over and corners him and starts telling jokes and funny stories at a furious clip. He's the pride of the inn. He's an author who has written countless books for boys and knows everything. He's full of ideas and fun and games.

But he gets on Herbert Johnson's nerves. The lonely man can't take all that wit. And he gives up drinking his coffee at the historic inn even though he likes the place and likes the girl behind the counter.

The girl's name is Alice. He often thinks of her. She has round arms and puff sleeves and a white apron. And she has cheerful eyes and such a nice laugh.

[35]

THERE'S NEVER ANY MAIL for Herbert Johnson. Nobody in the whole world writes to him. He's outside the system. He hasn't received a single letter from America either.

The mailman and Jens Jensen have often talked about it. It's really rather mysterious. He didn't even get so much as a card at Christmas. Surely there must be somebody who knows him. A man just can't be completely without relatives!

On the whole there's a lot that's peculiar about this Mr. Johnson. Not that he... after all, he is very quiet. But he's just a little too polite. He tips his hat when he meets people. There's something shifty about him. And where do you suppose he got all his money? He probably committed some crime over there in America.

That's what the well-digger's wife thinks too. On that very first day when she saw him walking by on the road, she thought there was something eerie about him. Something *sinister*. She's never talked to him, but she openly states her firm conviction that he must have killed somebody and that he's hiding from the police out here. She doesn't keep this theory to herself. She tells it to everybody she comes in contact with.

Even Hageholm has finally become convinced that there's something funny about the American. He said so to Jens Jensen too. "A man who never goes to church! He wasn't even in church on Christmas Eve. When you haven't got God, things are pretty bad." He doesn't understand why a man like Jens Jensen would want someone like that living in his house.

Herbert Johnson doesn't subscribe to any newspapers either. He doesn't know what's going on in the world. Great and significant things have happened that he doesn't have the slightest notion about. The Royal Theater is performing, and he doesn't know what works they're presenting and what the critics think about them. People are going abroad and coming home; an actor has traveled to Bornholm; several executives have celebrated anniversaries with their companies, and the newspapers haven't brought him word of any of it.

Once a month the mailman brings him a little local newspaper. But it's practically nothing but advertisements concerning breeding bulls and brood eggs and poems about the season and the Creator. And: "WARNING: If Jesper Nielsen curses at my wife again, I'll take him to court." And: "If Peter Andersen's dog does any more wandering around on property belonging to me, it will promptly be shot!"

He doesn't even have a radio to keep him informed of the events in the world and of the comings and goings of the Royal Family.

But Jens Jensen's radio is so powerful that he can't help hearing about world events through his wall.

"The Slangerup railroad line carried 4,200 passengers yesterday. At the swimming meet in the Frederiksberg swimming hall Ragnhild Hveger set a new Danish women's record in the

300-meter backstroke with a time of... His Majesty the King arrived in Slagelse today. The King was in radiant humor and greeted the mayor and the veterans' clubs and members of the rifle association who were there to meet him with their banners... Former hotelier Rasmussen of Holstebro is dead at the age of 82..."

The important news of the world reaches him through the wall with the Chinese moderne wallpaper. "Huddersfield defeated Cambridge yesterday, four goals to three. The boxing meet in Hermod attracted a large number of spectators. Spirits were high, and the bouts were first-class. In the welterweight division Aage Nielsen defeated Svend Asmundsen on points. In the flyweight division..."

Thank God for radio.

"The Crown Prince and Crown Princess visited the cheese exhibit in the Fyn Forum today... We will now have a discussion with the chairman of the Danish Wrestling Association."

In the evening Herbert Johnson sits on the bad springs of his overstuffed chair. The kerosene lamp with its brass ornamentation and glass fringe is lit. It's black and dark outside, and the wind is whistling noisily through the telephone poles and the old willow trees. He tends his woodstove using the new firewood he finally managed to get from the sawmill. He has gotten very good at stoking the fire even though it's not something he learned in school.

Through the wall his neighbor's radio brings him word from the outside world.

He isn't terribly interested. The events are transmitted out into space without making any impression on him. One day, however, there is something that catches his attention. He bolts up out of his chair and listens tensely. He puts his ear to the wall and listens and listens:

"People still remember the grisly suicide that occurred in October on Amager Common, where Head Clerk Teodor Amsted blew himself up with dynamite. At that very same time another man, 46-year-old Mikael Mogensen, disappeared from his home on Rosengade.

"The police have continued working on the case and have now received confirmation of their theory that the two men knew each other and that in some way there was a connection between their simultaneous disappearances. A former head teacher at the Metropolitan School, H. Schøff, recently informed the police that Teodor Amsted and Mikael Mogensen were classmates. The police have further established that there was some connection between them right up until Amsted's grisly death and Mogensen's disappearance. The possibility has not been ruled out that a criminal act may be involved. In reply to a question from the Radio News Department, however, Police Superintendent Tage Haderslev would reveal only that the police are actively working on the case and that they hope to have some results soon.

"The police have offered a reward of 500 kroner to anyone who can provide information about the missing Mikael Mogensen, who was last seen in October in his lodgings on Rosengade.

"Mikael Mogensen's description is as follows..."

[36]

THE TEMPERATURE HAS BEEN below freezing for several days. The windows are drafty, and the floors are cold in Herbert Johnson's little living room. The firewood disappears in the woodstove, but it doesn't really give off any heat. At night he freezes. Frost practically seems to form on his sheets and his heavy comforter.

The wind has started to pick up from the southeast. It's beginning to snow too. He stands at his window and follows the development of the weather with interest. There's going to be a real blizzard. The snow is drifting and blowing, and the ditches are filling up with snow. It's piling up in swaths across the road.

He watches it with a certain pleasure. When he was a boy, he loved it when it snowed. He would stand at the window in the evening and watch it drifting in the small round circle of light from the gas streetlights — it would be marvelous if there was so much snow that the streetcars couldn't run!

Strictly speaking he has no personal interest in snowy weather now. He's 46, and the time is long past when he threw snowballs or went sledding. Actually snowy weather doesn't concern him in the least. Nevertheless, he contemplates it with pleasure and follows its development anxiously, noting with satisfaction that it is picking up. The snow is getting thicker. The storm is getting stronger. The drifts across the road are growing. If things go on like this for long, traffic will come to a standstill.

There isn't much traffic to come to a standstill out here at this time of year. There's only the bakery truck and the butcher's truck that drive past Jens Jensen's house. And something called the Cheese Mart — a yellow truck full of cheeses and sausages and liver patés and a jovial driver. And of course there's Hageholm in his Ford, the restless soul.

There aren't any streetcars to come to a standstill. But the bus will have to give up trying to get through. And the little railroad line will have to shut down soon too. Or maybe the train will get stuck in the snow. Mr. Johnson is quite sad that he won't be taking the train tonight.

Next morning there are large snowdrifts on the ground. Cars are stuck in the snow here and there in the world. Jens Jensen's radio loudly proclaims rail stoppages and closed roads. No one has seen anything like this in living memory. It's worse than 1897!

Snow shovelers are at work on the road, young men wearing rubber boots and smoking pipes. Jens Jensen notes with distaste that they're playing and horsing around and throwing snow on each other and not doing any real work.

And of course there's an accident while they're working. It's nothing more than you might expect when people are horsing around and acting foolish. Something's bound to go wrong. One young man has three of his fingers crushed by a spade. Three fingers on his right hand. So he'll be an invalid for the rest of his life. But he was asking for it. So maybe next time he won't be so anxious to fool around!

The matter becomes even more serious. The gardener's son was the one who hit him with the spade. The gardener is Jens Jensen's bitter enemy. So Jens Jensen thoroughly interrogates everyone present, because here is finally an opportunity to nail the gardener.

Uh-huh, it happened while they were playing around. It's their own fault. The gardener's son will have to be liable for damages. If it had been an *accident,* then the town would have had to pay compensation. And those two guys probably knew that and talked it over and agreed to say that it *was* an accident. Now this is a serious matter, and Jens Jensen is fully aware of that fact. With great solemnity he picks up the telephone and reports to the police that, as far as he can see, this must be a case of false legal deposition. At most the gardener's son, not the town, will have to pay compensation. Otherwise it's up to the police to determine what further action is to be taken against the two young men who agreed to give a false statement.

A smile has appeared on Jens Jensen's stern countenance. He is in very high spirits when he tells Hageholm the story. Hageholm slaps his thigh in laughter. Hee hee hee! That serves them right. He starts up his Ford on the cleared road and drives out into the world to tell the news.

There is a lot of snow in the forest. Herbert Johnson sinks

down deep in it when he tries to step over the drifts. The branches of the fir trees have been bent all the way down to the ground by the snow. It looks strange and fantastic.

The hills are covered with snow and look like the Alps or Switzerland or Norway. On Sunday people come out and go skiing. Young girls in ski pants whoosh down the hills and glide through the white forest.

Those who live on the hills don't like having their untouched nature defiled by people. They look with anger and aversion at the skiing girls disturbing their solitude. They're happy when they manage to see a fox in the woods. A fox doesn't defile nature. But maybe it's people who don't belong in nature. The hill trolls emerge from beneath their thatched roofs making threatening gestures and shouting, "Can't you see the sign? Can't you read? This is PRIVATE PROPERTY!"

But the next day there is peace in the hills again. Now the young girls are sitting in their offices. No human beings disturb the trolls. They are at one with the foxes and the snow and nature.

[37]

A CAR STOPS IN FRONT of Jens Jensen's house.

Mr. Herbert Johnson looks at it with a certain uneasiness. There's something official about it that he doesn't like. He is anxious and nervous about everything that pertains to the authorities. He has a law degree, but he's afraid of the long arm of the law.

He has heard fragments of the news from Jens Jensen's radio that have brought anxiety and uneasiness into his life.

The authorities climb out of the car. Uniformed State Police officers are sitting inside it. The floor seems to sink beneath Mr. Johnson.

But there is no need for his heart to beat so violently. He can breathe easy. He's not the one whose number is up. Not this time.

Anders from the marsh is the one who's in trouble. He couldn't expect to get anything out of writing to the Ministry. Now the Parish Council's patience with him has run out. They've offered him work: "All right, there are plenty of rocks to crush!" But he only wants to collect relief money and be a burden on society. He's one of those people who have no shame.

As far as his house is concerned, it's no longer fit for human habitation, and they can't condone letting his three children live someplace where rain and snow come through the roof. It's been three months since he last paid the interest on his mortgage. There is a limit to everything.

A veritable motorcade drives down the narrow lane to Anders' house in the marsh. The car with the State Police officers. Jens Jensen and the chairman of the Parish Council and other members of the Social Welfare Committee. Hageholm, that restless soul, has also heard what's going to happen and is steering his car behind the others to Anders' place. He sits in his car shouting and directing things as if he were the actual leader of the expedition.

A couple of children are playing beside the house. They have a little windmill that's whirling in the brisk wind. Anders is good at making toys like that for his children.

They gaze at the approaching cars with interest. And Anders looks at the caravan with some surprise himself. He has a knife in his hand. He's whittling at something. An improved version of the windmill. A device that can raise and lower sacks. A little hoist just like the ones in real mills.

"He has a knife in his hand!" Hageholm screams. "Watch out!"

"Yeah, watch out!" the sheriff's deputy shouts. A State Police officer jumps out of the car and disarms the dangerous man.

The children look on in fright. Anders' wife comes out of the house. Alas, it's no fun being an authority and executing the law. But things must take their natural course. The quicker it's over with, the less painful it will be.

So Anders is transported to the penitentiary for hard labor.

He really isn't a big-time criminal. Not a dangerous person. But he's "afraid of work," to the extent that he refused to crush rocks on the beach. He's been a headstrong person and has caused Jens Jensen and the Parish Council a lot of trouble.

What the future has in store for him will depend on his own behavior. With good, submissive conduct, hard work, and obedience he might succeed in gaining the warden's favor. It's the warden of the institution who, in due time, can recommend Anders for parole.

The little windmill whirls in the wind in front of the empty house. Hageholm starts his car and drives off to tell everybody he meets what happened. "He had a knife in his hand, and if I hadn't seen it and shouted bloody murder, well, who knows what might have happened."

The parish will take care of Anders' wife and children. The Child Welfare Agency has had its eye on Anders' children for a long time. Jens Jensen is a member of the agency and he sees to it that the matter is taken care of. The two older children are dispatched to good, Christian homes where they'll be well brought up and learn how to do something productive.

The youngest child can stay with his mother. The town assigns her a small room. And Jens Jensen personally writes a requisition to his friend, the grocer, so she'll be able to buy 10 kroner's worth of goods. The people who run the town aren't monsters. Even if they were, the law has erected a protective shield in front of every single member of society. But they'll soon find out whether she's afraid of work too or whether she's willing to accept the work offered at "the prevailing wages of the local region."

[38]

THERE ARE MANY THINGS that can alarm and worry the solitary man who has rented rooms at Jens Jensen's house.

It's not just cars with State Police officers in them. It's not just census forms or tax notices or Jens Jensen's radio. There are a lot of other things that inspire him with a feeling of dread.

For instance, there's a small wad of banknotes that's getting smaller and smaller. There's a lottery jackpot that certainly can't last forever. And then what? There are still a lot of bills in the pile. But what about ten years from now?

Life has lost its security. There is no longer any pension beckoning reassuringly up ahead. The future is no longer something that is guaranteed and planned and laid out in advance.

This is a painful situation for a man for whom everything had always been carefully arranged, up to and including his funeral insurance.

He wanted to try being free. But it isn't so easy to administer your own freedom. You can't all of a sudden navigate your way around in life independently when you've always been taken in tow.

Everything has grown uncertain. Dangers and risks lurk everywhere. What will happen if he gets sick? And what will he do if somebody breaks in and takes a certain pile of money? And what if he's attacked? Or murdered?

He lies awake at night listening for footsteps out on the road. There are owls that hoot and cats that scream like babies. There are noises and horrible things out there in the dark.

He thought that he loved nature. But nature isn't as good as he learned in school. Nature isn't just Fure Lake and sunsets and pale green beech branches.

A fox steals into Jens Jensen's chicken yard and tears away at the birds with unimaginable cruelty. A cat plays with a mouse; it has bitten a leg off it so it can only run in circles. Ichneumon wasps eat their way out through a living larva. There is no end to the murder and mayhem in the marshes, woods, and fields.

Nature isn't the gentle mother that the poets of his Danish class sang about. And life in the country isn't the same as taking a summer vacation as a boy. "Tralalalalala, tralalalalala! Exalted as we travel with the peasant's load!" That was what they sang at the end-of-the-year ceremonies at the Metropolitan School.

Life in the country doesn't correspond to the picture he had of it in the city.

"God made the country, but man made the town," was how it went in an English poem he learned in school. The country was "groves that were to comfort the tired wanderer with their shadows."

But the country is also small houses whose windows are never opened. It is also dampness and dankness and rheumatism and bent backs and rubber boots and bunions and varicose veins. It is also pickled herring and roast pork rind seven days a week and vitamin deficiencies and stomach abscesses.

They look so quaint, these small houses with their thatched roofs and hedges and elder bushes and friendly little windows. But behind the windows people sit hating each other. And they're not really all that sorry when things go badly for someone else.

The houses have geraniums and charming little curtains. But there is also a lot of gloom and discomfort in those low-ceilinged living rooms. Odd and suspicious things go on there. What *did* happen when Jens Jensen's wife died? And Hageholm's? You don't hear about divorces out here. But you hear about other things. "Maybe it was a good thing that she died," they say. "He wasn't very good to her."

On the beach men sit splitting stones. They hammer and splinter them, and the chips pile up in huge heaps. There's a cold, damp wind blowing in from the sea. And somebody is coughing and spitting blood. Sometimes someone smashes his hand too. Chipping stones is not exactly healthy. And it's not supposed to be, either.

This isn't the same seashore where a properly supervised Herbert Johnson splashed around and dug in the sand with a little shovel as a child. The damp sea fog drifts in from the Kattegat so he freezes in his winter overcoat.

The fishing village is empty and deserted. The fishermen are staying indoors. The shop with bathing caps and bathing suits and rubber animals is closed. The kiosk has been shuttered up. Slushy snow is lying on the roof of the ice cream stand. The blue, red, green, and yellow bathing huts stand on the beach cold and forsaken. But on the shore by the parking lot men sit hunched over and wet, chipping stones in the rainy mist.

It gets dark early. Lamps are lit in the small houses. Some people go to bed because they have to ration their kerosene. But some people have bright electric lights that shine out onto the road.

And some people turn on their radios to hear lectures or old dance music or folksy waltz tunes and Danish ballads. People are sitting in their houses snug and contented, looking out for themselves.

But outside on the country road it's tremendously dark. One night a woman is attacked out there in the darkness. People hear a shrill scream. They go over to the windows in their little houses but they can't see anything. It's so absolutely, impenetrably black out there. There are several more screams. And then there's silence. And they pull the curtains shut and give the key a good twist in the lock. Because something certainly must be terribly wrong out there. Perhaps someone was being killed. Ugh, it sounded gruesome. It's best to lock the door. People are looking out for themselves.

The next day they talk about the girl who was attacked. Well, she was certainly asking for it. What was she doing running around out on the road at 8:30 at night anyway? She was probably going dancing at the inn. Could be she's what they call "man crazy." Yes, you should keep a good distance from somebody like that. You shouldn't get mixed up in anything. It's nobody else's business what goes on out there in the dark.

People look out for themselves.

Sometime in February a man from over on the other side of the marsh breaks through the ice and falls into a peat bog. He had been out cutting reeds for his roof. But the ice wasn't strong enough, and he went through. He lies there for some time calling for help. A man is passing by up on the road and hears him. And this man hurries home for a ladder.

He doesn't waste any time. He runs for all he's worth, as is his duty. But when he comes back with the ladder, the man is gone. He went under.

Maybe he could have tried to save him without a ladder. But of course that would have been risky. People look out for themselves.

Herbert Johnson sits at home making sure that the brass lamp with the decorations and the glass fringe doesn't smoke. He is sitting at his oval table. The table mat and the centerpiece with the ceramic apples have been shoved aside, and he's playing solitaire on the bare tabletop. No great intellectual interests occupy his mind. He has the normal, well-rounded education guaranteed by the university qualifying examination. He has studied Old Norse and Cæsar's Gallic Wars and Oehlenschlæger and plane geometry and world history. Later on, law and political economics and statistics were added. But there was never time for great cultural interests.

Someplace on Herluf Trollesgade there's a stamp collection. That was his main interest once. But he doesn't have access to it anymore. Now he has only a small box with coffee labels and pictures from advertisements to putter with.

And he plays solitaire. If it works out, fine. If it doesn't work out, no irreparable harm has been done. He can just try again.

[39]

ONE DAY THE AIR is a little different than usual. It's still cold, but there's something special about the wind. People sniff at the breeze and have a peculiar feeling of well-being. Spring is on its way.

Some faint new fragrances have arrived that people didn't notice during the winter. Something has happened to the soil that makes it smell different. And there are new sounds. The sparrows beside the house are chirping vigorously. Out over the fields you can hear the larks. And one afternoon you hear a starling. Just a few isolated trills that give you a strangely sweet and melancholy feeling.

Herbert Johnson has found the first little short-stemmed yellow coltsfoot by the roadside ditch. He is quite moved and puts it in the buttonhole of his winter overcoat. He feels happy and thankful. He walks along humming, swinging his walking stick a little.

Then the sun disappears. A strange coldness settles over the world. Herbert Johnson isn't humming anymore but is gripped by a profound sadness.

It is the first hint of spring.

Jens Jensen is a pessimistic man. He eyes nature with some anxiety. It's not good for spring to come so early. There's bound to be a repercussion. And that won't be so good. There's bound to be a lot that'll be ruined in people's gardens, and things like that.

There's frost during the night. But the fields have begun to turn quite green. "You can sure feel how strong the sun is now," people say. There are showers and hailstorms. But spring unfolds in spite of it all. You can hear the lapwings shrieking down in the marsh. At night you can hear the sounds of migrating birds.

There's a sense of restlessness in the air. And Hageholm is more restless than other people. He's bustling and fussing with innumerable things. He paints his picket fence and pounds nails in it and makes an awful racket. He digs up his garden like a madman. He is seized with panic. Fat Johanne is commandeered to do garden work too, and he shouts and screams at her.

He starts in too early on everything. The impatient man sows his peas a month before anyone else. And when they come up, they get frostbitten and turn black. And then everything has to be done all over again. He's a restless soul.

But spring is unfolding. And the time comes when other people begin to dig and sow in their gardens too. Snowdrops and little blue scillas come up, and the winter aconites are already gone.

Herbert Johnson follows the developments in Jens Jensen's garden. And he thinks about a grave in Assistens Cemetery. Now they're fixing and raking it too. And he's sure that they're setting pots with tall, melancholy Easter lilies into the ground. One pot on each side of the gravestone.

Karen has started work in the garden too. When she's out

there bending over, she's quite nice to look at. When she's got her back turned, you can't see her sour face. Herbert Johnson notices that she's well-built and has a nice figure and round legs. He's sure that she must be firm and pleasant to the touch. But he's not the passionate type. And he knows that Jens Jensen will keep a close watch on his daughter's virtue.

Jens Jensen is a serious man. He is opposed to any form of frivolity or dissipation. He can be seized by anger when he sees the pigeons out in the farmyard. There are males that puff themselves up and become incredibly wild and foolish, so it's disgusting to look at. Jens Jensen is indignant and throws things at them and claps his hands. By God, that's no way to behave! That's not something for Karen to see. She might get all kinds of ideas from that. And then when you have one of those Americans living in your house. You never know what a person like that might think of. He probably tried a little of everything with the Indians over there. But just let him try anything here! We'll teach him a thing or two!

Jens Jensen gives his lodger a dark look.

[40]

SPRING HASN'T MADE PEOPLE any less cantankerous.

They report each other to the police for a variety of things and want to have the book thrown at each other. After all, when there's a law it's supposed to be obeyed, isn't it?

Some dogs have been running around loose. According to the law, they're supposed to be kept under control. Of course nothing serious happened this time. But who knows what might have happened? What if one of those mutts charges out onto the road after a bicycle? "Yep, that's pretty bad, all right," says the local police officer over the telephone.

The forester's spotted dog has paid a nocturnal call on the well-digger's black dog. So what are the puppies going to look like? These are grounds for a lawsuit and damages. Of all people the forester ought to know that he's got no right to let his dog roam around loose. "We'll look into the matter," says the officer.

There are people who can't control themselves, and who shoot their guns despite the clear provisions of the hunting regulations. They're reported too. "That's awful," the policeman replies.

Hageholm is a zealous man and an untiring informant. He reports to the police officer that there can't be any doubt that it's his old adversary, the bicycle mechanic, who is hunting in the marsh illegally. But there's no proof, and the police are powerless to do anything to the bicycle mechanic.

But then the bicycle mechanic takes an odd form of revenge. After Hageholm has driven off to the cemetery with Johanne, he sneaks into his yard and relieves himself, both ways, on Hageholm's freshly painted white lawn furniture. It would be hard to match such disgusting behavior. This is reported, naturally, but the police can't do anything without absolute proof. "Yep, that's pretty bad, all right," says the officer.

Twice a week Martin Hageholm drives to the little cemetery in the woods where his wife and daughter are buried. He rakes and putters around and spreads beach gravel on the grave. And he dries off the brass chains with a cloth.

Johanne is always with him. Nobody knows what she thinks about when she decorates Mrs. Hageholm's grave. She doesn't say a thing, but twitches her mouth and blinks her little eyes.

Hageholm's prospective son-in-law has married someone else, barely a year after his fiancée's death. That's just like him; so that's all the impression it made on him. Yet he does come out every so often to put flowers on her grave.

But Hageholm isn't about to put up with that. He takes the young man's flowers and flings them far away. "They were wilted!" Hageholm says when he complains about it. "You've got a new wife anyhow. She ought to be enough for you."

A bitter dispute erupts between the two men.

"It's my grave!" says Hageholm. "I already bought and paid for it for my wife. I've renewed it and paid for a granite monument and brass chains."

"But it's my corpse!" the young man counters. And if anyone tries to prevent him from putting flowers on the grave, he can have the corpse dug up and moved to another grave.

But Hageholm is holding a trump card in his hand. His daughter died of tetanus. Who knows whether she might still be contagious down there? They say those *bac-silluses* can stay alive for nine years.

Hageholm calls up the county doctor and inquires whether permission can be given to dig up the corpse since it has tetanus and might still be contagious.

The county doctor doesn't think so. "No, you'd better just leave it alone. Why should it be dug up?"

Hageholm has won.

Herbert Johnson is a peaceful man. He doesn't get together with anyone socially. There are no possibilities for conflict. But he hears what goes on.

His landlord has his worries too. Jens Jensen is a serious and conscientious man. But he too is subject to abuse and annoyances, just when he thought that Anders was safely incarcerated in the workhouse with no chance of making any more trouble.

But Anders has no doubt also noticed that it's spring and wouldn't mind getting out again. He knows that when a man has committed a crime, his case will be brought before the bench. He will get a defense attorney, and the decision can be appealed to a higher court. Everything takes place in public and under scrutiny.

But Anders is no criminal. He has merely refused to split the town's stones because he felt that the pay was too low. And now he's locked up for an indefinite period.

The only thing they can allow him to do is write a letter to the county and try to explain his case. Anders isn't much of a writer, but he manages to finish a letter. And the head clerk at the county courthouse who receives his halting letter forwards it to Jens Jensen with an inquiry.

Now it's Jens Jensen's turn to put things in writing. He isn't much of a penman either, and he is filled with rage toward this Anders who won't leave him in peace. It takes him time to put together a letter, but from this letter it is evident that the aforesaid Anders is afraid of work and given to drink and unable to fulfill his duty to provide for his family. The head clerk at the county courthouse laboriously works his way through the letter and concludes that no injustice has been done to Anders.

Now Anders can try his luck again by writing a letter to the Ministry of Social Affairs. But he'd do better to try to win the favor of the warden of the institution, who has control over when he'll be released.

Jens Jensen's bad humor also affects his tenant. It comes to his attention that the wallpaper has been ripped. That sort of vandalism will have to be paid for. And as far as varnishing the floors is concerned, that's something the tenant is responsible for. Mr. Johnson has by now paced back and forth so much that the floor is completely worn. But Jens Jensen isn't going to stand there and let his apartment decrease in value. Now the matter of varnishing will have to be straightened out if Mr. H. Johnson wishes to be permitted to go on living there. Summer is on the way, and there are plenty of people who would like to rent an apartment out here!

How he goes about doing the varnishing is something Jens Jensen doesn't intend to get involved in. But he's big and strong and certainly ought to be able to varnish a floor. Otherwise there are workers he can hire. And of course it's also possible that Karen might be willing to take on the varnishing for a modest fee.

That's the way it finally works out. The rip in the wallpaper is glued up as well. Herbert Johnson will be able to go on living out here and continue his new life.

[41]

JENS JENSEN'S TENANT has suddenly started working on some mysterious and secretive projects.

People observe his conduct with curiosity and speculate about what the American might be up to. He didn't do a single thing all winter. He idled his time away so it was thoroughly disgusting to watch. But now he's suddenly been seized by a strange burst of activity.

He comes home from the grocery store with large packages. And he unpacks them with a secretive expression on his face. The packages contain large mason jars, which he places on the windowsill. Both Jens Jensen and Karen observe his industry with amazement.

Herbert Johnson buys himself a little net on the end of a pole. He goes out to catch things in the marsh and the river. It doesn't take long before Hageholm comes down to have a closer look at this fishing. He merely wishes to inform Mr. Johnson that he's the one who has the fishing rights in this part of the river. As far as the other parts are concerned, it depends on what the individual owners have to say. Any pike that might happen to be in the peat bogs or marsh pools belong to specifically identified persons. But Mr. Johnson isn't out after fish at all. He isn't infringing on anybody's property rights. He only catches salamanders, tadpoles, and aquatic insects in his net. Neither Hageholm nor anyone else can have anything against that, can they? "Just as long as it doesn't interfere with the fish breeding," says Hageholm.

He sets up small aquariums in the mason jars. He puts aquatic plants and sand and small stones into them. Ram's-horn snails wander up and down the sides of the jars keeping them free of algae.

Dragonfly larvae and water scorpions are plopped into the jars as they are caught in the American's net. Strange and unusual animals with cilia and mandibles. Animals that breathe through their abdomens, and animals that always lie on their backs. Caddis worms in strange shells and water beetles and polyps.

Now the news leaks out that the American is actually one of those naturalist types. That must be the reason he's a freethinker and never attends church. People have to wonder that a man like Jens Jensen would care to have someone like that living in his house—but of course, he does pay him well. Nobody can resist that. Not even Jens Jensen.

Herbert Johnson sits looking at his animals. These small aquariums are a wish of his that he has finally managed to fulfill, and he is absolutely ecstatic.

As a child he always wanted an aquarium, but his mother wouldn't permit it. That sort of thing was far too messy. He'd do better to concentrate on his homework. When he was grown-up and could afford to buy aquariums himself, his wife was opposed to the idea. "That really isn't something for a grown man! And all the mess it makes. Those things smell bad, you know!"

When he was a child, he was given a fishing net every year. But he was forbidden to fish for anything with it. He might drown in the marsh pools, and he could get filthy in the ditches and puddles. He was only allowed to fish at the beach because there wasn't anything to catch there.

But now he has managed to fulfill his wish. He's 46 years old now. Almost 47. He's too late for everything.

He sits and observes life in the mason jars.

There are animals that lie lurking at the bottom and extend complex grasping apparatuses toward other animals. They eat each other in the jars. They suck each other's blood, leaving only an empty shell behind. They slash each other to pieces and maim each other so it's horrible to behold. The water spiders rise and descend like small silver droplets. When a water cricket comes close to them, they spin a web around it and suck out its blood. The big animals eat the smaller animals. And the smallest animals eat creatures that are so tiny you can't even see them.

Herbert Johnson looks on with a shudder. The nature lover contemplates nature with horror.

Every day he brings home some new prize to his jars. Notonectids, daphnias, sticklebacks. He is seized by the eagerness of the hunter. It's the springtime that is affecting the solitary man.

And spring unfolds.

Nature is now filled with an abundance of life and activity. There's a nightingale living in Jens Jensen's yard. Other nightingales living down in the marsh answer it when it starts singing in the evening. The night is full of sounds. There are a whole lot of things happening in the yard and the marsh.

The nights are bright and pale and strange. The fog lies low so the marsh resembles a lake.

There are peeping, snorting, and snuffling sounds. The hedgehogs are grunting with love and chasing each other. The frogs are making a racket in the marsh. They sound like thousands of castanets. The wild geese are honking. The moor hens are cackling. Things are crawling, scurrying, and bustling everywhere.

Herbert Johnson stands and listens to all this noise in the evening. He stands by the blue gate and looks out across the white marsh where all this energy is unfolding. Mosquitoes buzz around his head and suck some of his blood.

He can't sleep at night because of all the din from the nightingales and frogs. Long before sunup a cuckoo starts to sing like a lunatic. It's sitting in the bushes and cuckooing in through his bedroom window. It sings out several hundred years of life to him.

All the animals are crazy during this season.

But the humans aren't quite right in the head either.

Martin Hageholm, that zealous man, is an expert at ferreting out loving couples and creeping up on them unawares and chasing them apart. "It's disgusting the way they carry on!"

He can see them from the top of the hill with his hunting binoculars and observe their activities. He sneaks up on them and surprises them right in the middle of it all. "May I please have your name and address!" he shouts furiously. If they're strangers who don't know him, they may think he's a policeman. And he solemnly writes it all down in a little notebook. "Now you've been *written up*! You'll be hearing from me!" he says darkly.

He tells Johanne about the shocking things he's seen. "Would you believe it? *She* was lying on top of him! Why, the world's turned upside down! Hee hee hee!"

"No, people aren't quite right in the head anymore," she says. "To think that they have no shame." And Johanne twitches her mouth as if she wanted to say something more.

The countryside looks so peaceful. But it is rife with more things than you'd think possible.

Why, for instance, do you think that the Cheese Mart truck has to be parked for hours over at the edge of the woods? What do you think the driver is doing?

Hageholm can report that one of the fine ladies from up in the hills is shacking up with the Cheese Mart man. That's the way those ladies from Copenhagen are!

But that's going too far, and we won't stand for it. Hageholm picks up the phone and calls the store in town. Now the owner of the Cheese Mart will find out what his driver is up to in the woods.

But you can still see the truck parked at the edge of the woods every day, to everyone's indignation and disgust. They obviously couldn't care less at the store in town. The lascivious Cheese Mart man can carry on any way he likes.

[42]

IT'S GETTING WARM. People are complaining about the dry weather. If it keeps up like this, there'll be crop failures. There won't be any sugar beets, and the grain won't germinate. No one has seen anything like it in living memory.

There are no more firewood problems for Herbert Johnson. Now it's the flies that plague him. But he has figured out how to hang up flypaper beside the hanging lamp. And he's proud of his ingenuity and practical sense.

The snails in his aquarium are laying great clusters of eggs. The water spiders have had babies and have eaten them. The mason jars are teeming and swarming with activity, and the most horrible things are happening inside them.

People are starting to come out here on Sundays. The hill dwellers get their signs painted. The vipers are coming out of the heather and lying on the paths to sun themselves. The nature conservationists gaze at them affectionately.

This is the time of year when country people are encouraged to take in a child from Copenhagen for vacation. Boys are especially hard to place.

Jens Jensen won't be having a vacation girl. He has Karen, after all. She's healthy and strong and can certainly do what needs to be done around the house. There's no reason to provide food for one more person.

But Hageholm's Johanne is old and not as well as she used to be. He writes for a vacation girl. And it has to be one from the upper grades. Johanne puts off doing the laundry until the girl arrives. And the spring cleaning. Then the time will come, of course, for canning and preserving. There will be plenty for Hageholm's vacation girl to do.

Cars are starting to appear on the road. The milkman and the baker and the butcher and the Cheese Mart and restless Hageholm aren't the only ones anymore. Truck farmers also appear with fresh radishes, and men selling brushes, and people looking for apartments for the summer.

Vacation season is about to begin.

There are earwigs living in the holes of Herbert Johnson's bath sponge. Spiders spin long threads from the ceiling and climb up and down above his bed. And the flies hang on the flypaper buzzing and buzzing and take a long time to die.

This was the time of year when he used to take his examinations. He has taken so many exams that it's in his blood. He can't experience spring anymore without feeling oppressed. Spring is the time when you're supposed to study and review and prepare. The first days of summer are exam days. The sensation was the same in high school and at the university. Sunshine and warmth and lilacs — these meant the annual examination and the risk of failure. That's the way it was from the time he was seven years old until he was 25. Every single spring was stolen from him. Then later Leif's exams came along. The whole thing all over again with anxiety and studying and agitation. Summer and studying for exams and nervousness all go together.

It's very hot underneath Jens Jensen's comforters. The weather is muggy and ominous. There must be a thunderstorm brewing. Something has to happen. Maybe it will blow over this time. But sooner or later the catastrophe will come. Herbert Johnson knows this.

He listens to Jens Jensen's radio news every evening. He puts his ear to the brown wallpaper and listens to find out whether anything is mentioned about a certain Head Clerk Amsted and a ghastly suicide on Amager Common and a missing eccentric from Rosengade.

It's been some time since they mentioned anything about it on the radio. But the police are working on the case. Perhaps a few surprises can still be expected. It's difficult to fall asleep at night. It doesn't really get dark anymore. And it's so muggy and close in his cramped rooms.

Sometimes he gets up at 4 o'clock and looks after his aquariums and plays the day's first games of solitaire.

Early one morning a girl comes walking along out on the road. She's a young, pretty girl. But her hair is a mess, and she looks disheveled. She has thrown up on the road and she can hardly walk.

Jens Jensen is up early too. He knows the girl very well. It's the girl from over at the "historic" inn. She's probably been out partying. Some farmhands probably got her drunk and had their fun fooling around with her.

She stops and leans up against the blue gate. "Please, Mr. Jensen! Couldn't I use your telephone to call down to the inn? I can hardly walk anymore."

"My telephone's not for people like you!"

"Then couldn't *you* call and just ask Ole to come out here in his car and pick me up?"

"There won't be any telephone calls from my house for people like you!"

"Yes, but I'll pay you for it."

"Just get moving, will you, and let go of my gate! We don't

want any of your puke on the railing. I can tell you that the inn's that way. It's exactly 4 kilometers. It'll do you good to use your legs for walking too!"

So the girl from the inn staggers off into the early summer morning.

Herbert Johnson saw her from his window and heard what was said. He also knows the girl well. She gave him a nice smile when he drank his afternoon coffee down at the inn. Her name is Alice.

He has a good mind to invite her inside now, so she can rest a little. He would also like to give her some headache powder and some coffee and pay for a taxi for her.

But he doesn't dare do it because of Jens Jensen. He doesn't dare risk displeasing his landlord.

He doesn't have the capacity to commit independent or rebellious acts.

[43]

IT'S SUMMER AND vacation time. Down in the fishing village the hotel and the *pensions* have opened. The fishermen move out to their sheds and let the people from Copenhagen have their houses.

"Has your riff-raff arrived?" one fisherman's wife asks another.

"No, our riff-raff won't be coming until Saturday."

The shop owners put fresh merchandise on their shelves. Now they have to make the money they're going to live on for the rest of the year.

The fishing village is swarming with sun-tanned young people.

Men in blue and yellow polo shirts. And pretty girls with bare brown backs and colored scarves. And there are older people with sunglasses and Panama hats and parasols.

The fishermen stand leaning up against their houses and boats and spit long streams after the strangers.

Hageholm's vacation girl is busy beating the green plush easy chairs that have been moved out into the yard. She cleans and brushes comforters, mattresses, and winter clothing. Things have to be scoured and scrubbed too, and the stairs in front of the house have to be washed off with sudsy water. But the girl is big and strong, and it won't hurt her to do a little work.

Crowds of bathers are splashing in the water at the beach. People are lying in the dunes being baked by the sun.

The water is so green and clear and tempting. Herbert Johnson decides to buy a bathing suit. Why shouldn't he go swimming and enjoy life now that he's here anyway?

He has been to the beach and is walking home through the woods. Hardly anybody ever walks along the sandy paths here. It's so burning hot here in the forest. It smells of resin and pine needles. House flies and mosquitoes and warble flies buzz around his head. He has to keep waving his handkerchief to be able to stand it.

The forest is enormous. A person can get lost in it. There is a plantation of pine trees, and heather and sand. But there are also cool places, with tall, soft grass. There are juniper bushes that look like cypress trees. And white birch trees and pale green larches. And there is a dark, cool beech forest.

Long, straight fire lanes have been carved through the woods. There are lanes that run the entire length of the forest. From a high place you can see for miles down one of these lanes.

"Lord knows where it ends. Someday I really ought to follow it and see where it comes out."

Herbert Johnson has thought about this before. But nothing has ever come of it. Nothing will ever come of it.

He returns to his house along the protected path through the hills which Dr. Ejegod has given him permission to walk on.

There are a couple of cars parked in front of the house. One of them is Hageholm's Ford, of course.

Hageholm is standing on the road with several other people.

"There he is!" Hageholm shouts, pointing at Herbert Johnson. "Watch out! There he is!"

"Hello, *Teodor Amsted*," says a man. A man wearing a windbreaker and bicycle clips. "So, it's out here you've been hiding."

"Watch out for him!" Hageholm screams. "Just watch out that he doesn't run away!"

"He won't be running anywhere," says an officer. He takes Herbert Johnson by the arm and holds him firmly.

The arrested man looks around...

He looks at the blue picket fence. And he sees Hageholm and Jens Jensen and Karen and several unfamiliar men.

The whole thing is like a dream. It's as if it had nothing to do with him.

In his window there are several mason jars with snails and algae and cruel aquatic insects. But of course they'll be taken care of too.

Teodor Amsted lets things happen. He's used to having other people take the initiative. He's used to being administered.

The officer nudges him into the car. The door slams shut. The motor starts up.

Hageholm shakes his head. "Is that any way to arrest a man? He could have taken off a hundred times. Why didn't they have handcuffs with them?"

Hageholm is all blue in the face from exasperation. He starts off for town and the jail to find out what's new. If they need a witness, why, he's at their service!

And maybe there was a *reward* posted for the apprehension of the criminal. Hageholm intends to lay claim to it. Because he always thought there was something fishy about that American. Didn't he even say so to Jens Jensen and the others? "So if there's any talk of a reward..."

Hageholm races down the country road in his Ford. He's a restless soul.

PART THREE

[44]

THERE IS A YOUNG MAN sitting in Head Clerk Amsted's apartment on Herluf Trollesgade.

A slender young man with a pretty face. He is sitting in one of the leather easy chairs in the study beside the Turkish smoking table. He isn't smoking, though. He can't tolerate tobacco smoke. He mustn't partake of alcoholic spirits either. That would destroy his special powers.

The young man is the medium Einer Olsen, who has been the intermediary between Mrs. Amsted and her husband.

Everything has remained unchanged in the apartment. Teodor Amsted's portrait is sitting in its leather frame on the shiny card table looking rather shyly out into the room. He has two worried wrinkles on his forehead.

The lighting in the study is subdued. It's almost like seance lighting. A yellowish-brown parchment shade with brocade and silk fringe is softening the light. Mrs. Amsted looks quite young in the pale, bronze-yellow light.

They're sitting in Teodor Amsted's den. And they're speaking about life and death, which is not a real death but only a transformation—a *transition*.

It was the poet, Mrs. Drusse, who brought the message to Mrs. Amsted from the spiritual world. But Mrs. Drusse doesn't come to Herluf Trollesgade anymore. The two women no longer see each other. Their warm friendship has turned into bitter animosity.

In the beginning it was purely religious matters that separated the two women. But there were more reasons later on. The gap between them is deep and unbridgeable.

Mrs. Amsted *has* accepted spiritualism. But her relationship to the Congregation was never as fervent or intimate as it was for Mrs. Drusse. Mrs. Amsted never formed close attachments to the Brothers and Sisters on Philippavej.

She took part in seances and learned how to use the spiritual apparatus which so ingeniously facilitates communication between the spirits who have "gone over" and those who still live on the earthly plane.

But she didn't attend the Temple regularly. She wasn't a faithful participant in the worship service and common prayers. She never recruited new Sisters and Brothers for the spiritualist cause. And she did not bestow upon the Congregation the financial support that could be expected of someone in her circumstances.

"Her use of spiritualism has been egoistic!" said Mrs. Drusse. "She is still full of the pride of this world. She is not a ministrant Sister but a hardened, thistle-like soul!"

These are harsh words. But they are not the harshest. The innuendoes and insinuations Mrs. Drusse has aired both to Damascus the printer and to Mrs. Amsted herself have been even more offensive and have made any association between the two women impossible.

No one in the Circle wished to deny the authenticity of the communications which Mrs. Amsted received from her husband through the medium. But Mrs. Drusse objected to the fact that frail young Olsen was always the connecting link. Why wasn't it ever possible to induce Teodor Amsted's spirit to send its messages through another medium, such as the very able female medium, Maja?

It was obvious that it was precisely Olsen who was attuned to the same spiritual tonality as Mrs. Amsted. But is it proper for one Sister to monopolize a medium's powers to such an extent that he is almost inaccessible to other spiritual beings? Isn't that a misuse of the powers that ought to serve the common good and not merely the private interests of one individual?

"We mediums are not happy people," Einer Olsen says. "We are so impressionable—so receptive—so hypersensitive... It's so strange to feel one's Brother Body possessed by an alien intelligence. One's own soul is homeless and quakes in fear of never being able to return. One grows so tired—so utterly exhausted..."

"Was the trance a strain on you?" Mrs. Amsted asks softly. And she strokes his blond hair like a mother. "Poor boy! Are you tired?"

"It's not that bad. Here, where the spiritual contact is so perfect... But in the Circle! Oh, sometimes it can actually be painful. It hurts so much when one feels that one of the Assembled is nurturing hostile thoughts. When the spiritual chain is not whole. If only all people knew how careful one must be with one's thoughts! And when two intelligences want to take up residence in my body at the same time! Like the time in the Temple when the table was smashed—my life was in extreme danger. I didn't think that my own soul would ever return to its Brother Body. It was horrible... One would think that at least those who have 'gone over' ought to be cleansed and purified and free from physical desire. But unfortunately there are far too many who continue to be as they were here on the earthly plane. I can wake up at night quivering with fear of that Hakon person and that Drusse—those two spirits who still have not attained the serenity and purity that are preconditions for life on the spiritual plane. With them I feel that it isn't love but a kind of lust that enters my Brother Body. There are impure wishes and desires defiling it... Oh, if you only knew how horrible it is!"

"Poor, poor boy! It must be hard for you. But things are better here, aren't they?"

"Oh yes, oh yes. Things are very different here. Here there is a kindred intelligence that takes up abode in the Brother Body. Here there is harmony. Here the instruments have been tuned to each other. It's as if... as if I were almost—myself."

"You're not that tired now?"

"No. Just a little bit. As long as I can just sit here and rest a little. There's such a sense of peace here."

"Isn't there anything you'd like? Tea or something like that?"

"No thank you. No. The Brother Body has had everything it needs. Ah, that was invigorating. There is so much wear on one's body that its need for material nourishment is greater than that of other people. But here it has received enough. It was invigorating. You cook wonderfully, Mrs. Amsted."

"Do you really think so? That makes me happy. I did go to a little extra trouble."

The clock in the dining room chimes. Slowly and solemnly. Eleven times.

"It's late now. But it's so nice to sit here. There's such a sense of peace here. It feels so good."

"Just rest. Rest as long as you like. Let this be like your own home. I owe you so terribly much . . . you and him."

"Don't you ever think of the future, Mrs. Amsted?" He has taken her hand and is looking at the lines on it.

"I don't know. Can you tell me about the future?"

"I could tell you a great deal. You will be happy. Even here on the earthly plane. Very, very happy. You will journey across a great body of water. And you will experience love. Pure, undefiled love . . ."

He has leaned forward and is looking attentively at her hand with its numerous fine lines. It is very quiet in the room.

And then suddenly they both give a start. A sharp, piercing bell breaks the silence, so that they cringe as if in fear.

Mrs. Amsted gets up and walks over to the telephone. "Now who can this be? At this hour? . . . Oh, it's almost spooky. I just hope it's not something about *Leif*! I've been so worried about him since he left for boarding school. A child shouldn't be separated from his mother. But of course it was necessary under these circumstances... Yes. Yes... hello... Who? What are you saying? The *police?*"

Olsen looks uneasily at Mrs. Amsted. He has gotten up and walked discreetly into the other room. But he is listening attentively and anxiously.

"Alive?... But of course I know that. He's alive. There is no such thing as death!... What did you say? My husband?... In North Sjælland? Arrested in North Sjælland?... Living under an assumed name? But—but... what *is* this? Oh God, what *is* this you're telling me? Oh, help me!...

"Olsen! Olsen!... Do you hear me? Help me! Something terrible has happened!"

She has dropped the telephone and is running in to Olsen.

But he is no longer in the living room. She hears his soft footsteps in the hallway. And she hears the front door slam.

The medium Einer Olsen has withdrawn.

[45]

Teodor Amsted doesn't have any time to rest after his automobile trip through North Sjælland.

There are so many things the police want to ask him about. There is so much they want to know. For almost a year they have been working on finding him. And now that they have him, he'll have to give them information about everything that is still obscure and puzzling.

He has no intention of hiding anything. He is used to answering questions. He has taken so many examinations that he really wants to answer everything correctly.

But he can't give an explanation for everything, even though he really wants to. There is a lot that is puzzling even to him. There were sudden impulses and fortuitous circumstances that he himself wasn't able to control. Things weren't as straightforward and premeditated and well prepared as the police assume.

"Why did you do it? Why did you want to disappear? Why did you pretend to commit suicide?"

It's not an easy question to answer. It was probably a small craving for freedom that was suddenly permitted to break through when fortuitous circumstances made it possible. He probably wanted to administer himself for once. He wanted to have control over himself, his time, his apparel, and his meals. But it's not all that easy to explain to the police.

"Wasn't your marriage a happy one?"

"Oh, yes, I guess it was."

"But how could it have been? A man doesn't just leave his wife if he's happy with her!"

"No."

So he was in love with another woman? He was having an extramarital affair?

"No. No." There had never been anyone else besides his wife.

But the police did find a poem, to a lady — to a kiosk lady. It was found during a search of his apartment on Herluf Trollesgade. How is he going to explain that?

"It's so long ago. It was quite childish. It has no significance whatsoever. None whatsoever."

"What was the lady's name?

He can't answer that. Now why should he cause trouble for an innocent kiosk lady? No, he doesn't remember what her name was.

But what did he and his wife quarrel about? Why did they have a falling-out?

They didn't quarrel. They never had a falling-out.

Well, then it must have been a put-up job. His wife knew about the plan. It was done to cash in on his life insurance policy!

No, no. His wife knew nothing about it. And he hadn't even thought about his life insurance.

"Listen, you've got to pull yourself together!" Police Superintendent Haderslev tells him. "You've got to answer my questions properly! Now think *very* carefully!"

Amsted thinks and thinks. But he is unable to devise an explanation that will satisfy the police superintendent.

"How much did you win in the lottery?"

"The lottery? Do you know about the lottery?"

"Yes, we know a lot more than you think. But would you answer, please!"

"The ticket was worth 50,000 kroner."

"I see. And it was a half ticket. So you received 25,000 kroner."

"Yes."

"Why did you keep this hidden from your wife?"

"I don't really know. It was so strange having this money. I didn't have any plans for it. I just put it away. I kept it in a drawer at the office—at the War Ministry."

"What do you mean you didn't have any plans? You lived on this money in the country, didn't you?"

"I hadn't decided to... to go to the country at the time I won the money."

"When did you decide to 'go to the country'?"

"It came all of a sudden. It was after Mogensen's suicide."

"You're certain that Mikael Mogensen committed suicide?"

"Yes. What else?"

"*You're* not the one who's supposed to be asking the questions. I'm asking you whether you're quite certain that Mogensen died of his own free will?"

"Yes, I am."

"You went to school with Mogensen?"

"Yes. To the Metropolitan School."

"And you continued to get together with him?"

"Just occasionally. I knew where he lived. And sometimes I sent him a little—a little help."

"Help? What kind of help? Help for what?"

"Mogensen was very poor. Once in a while I gave him a little money. And he got my old suits too. My wife thought that my suits were being given to a messenger at the office."

"Why wasn't your wife supposed to know that you knew Mogensen and were helping him?"

"I don't think she would have cared for him. He was very peculiar. He often said rather—rather drastic things. And he wasn't particularly well-groomed."

"Was there any special reason that you supported Mogensen financially?"

"No."

"So why did you do it then?"

"He was very poor."

"But there are an awful lot of poor people in Copenhagen. You certainly couldn't support them all. Why precisely Mogensen? Wasn't there some special reason?"

"No."

"So you simply got carried away by your kind heart?"

"I knew Mogensen, I told you. He was a classmate."

"How much money did you give Mogensen?"

"Just small amounts. It was only when I won the money in the lottery that I gave him a larger amount."

"How much is 'a larger amount'?"

"I gave him a thousand kroner from my lottery winnings."

"That was very generous. And there really wasn't any other reason for this generosity than compassion for an old classmate?"

"I thought that he should rent a better room. And get some new clothes. Then maybe he could get a job, too."

"So what did he use the money for?"

"I don't know—I mean—I'm afraid he probably used it to buy dynamite."

"But you can't just buy dynamite at the corner grocery store. How did he acquire the explosives?"

"I don't know."

"You were interested in explosives yourself, weren't you? You were reading big, thick books about explosives. Where did this interest come from?"

"It was purely professional. I mean, it concerned my work in the Ministry. We were working on a report regarding a project that had been submitted about so-called 'mechanical soldiers'—a kind of mine. And I was involved in drawing up the Ministry's report. So I had to acquaint myself with certain technical details."

"I see. You're quite certain that that's the way it is?"

"Yes. What else?"

"*I'm* the one asking the questions. Would you be so kind as to remember that!... It wasn't from some more *private* interest that you were studying explosives?"

"No, I didn't have any private interest in those items."

"It must be practically impossible for a man like Mogensen to get hold of dynamite. Don't you think so? What kind of contacts could he have had?"

"I don't know."

"You yourself, for instance, would have been able to acquire explosives far more easily, wouldn't you? When a person is supposed to be working on mines and 'mechanical soldiers' in an official capacity, it wouldn't be impossible to procure some dynamite, would it?"

"It wouldn't be that easy."

"Not even for you?"

"In any event it would only be possible in some criminal manner."

"I see. And a man like you would never engage in anything criminal?"

Teodor Amsted doesn't answer.

"In any case it would be far more difficult for Mikael Mogensen to acquire dynamite than you. Wouldn't it?"

"Well, yes."

"But you have no idea at all how Mogensen went about it?"

"No."

"Do you know whether Mogensen had been entertaining plans about suicide for a long time?"

"No—I don't know... well, yes, I guess he did sort of talk about it a few times. But it wasn't anything to take seriously."

"What did he say? Please answer precisely!"

"He talked about so many strange things. Things like renting an airplane and throwing himself out of it. Or a balloon and 'ascending to heaven.' Mogensen said so many things you really couldn't take seriously."

"When you left your office in Section 14 of the War Ministry for the last time, you had just received a letter. The letter came via messenger. Would you tell us who wrote the letter?"

"Mogensen did. He wrote about his suicide. That he was now in the process of executing his plan. He was going to blow himself up with dynamite out on Amager. It was a very alarming letter: 'Now I'm ascending to heaven. The rest of you can keep crawling around down here. I'm raising myself to a higher atmospheric stratum. Life means nothing to me. But I am dissatisfied with the forms that life takes. I am the last philosopher. I will die like a *Greek*.'"

"What kind of *Greeks* died that way?"

"Mogensen always expressed himself so strangely. He couldn't really subjugate himself to society. He was so good in high school. But after he graduated, things sort of came to a standstill for him."

"What did you do with the letter?"

"I tore it to pieces immediately after I got it."

"That's too bad. Then what did you do, after you had read Mogensen's eccentric message?"

"I left at once. For Amager Common. I hoped I'd get there in time."

"Why didn't you inform the police? Don't you think that a police squad car would have been able to get there faster?"

"Well, yes. That was my mistake. But I wasn't really sure if Mogensen was actually going to do it. He said things like that so often. And then I thought there would be more time. He wrote that he was walking out there right away. But the letter had been sent by messenger, so not much time could have passed. And I took a taxi."

"Thank you. We know that. We've talked to the driver. Your story checks out as far as that goes. Then what did you do?"

"I walked to the place that Mogensen had described. Where the embankment above Kalvebod Strand meets the Common. 'There you will find a hole in the ground,' Mogensen wrote."

"And what did you find?"

"There really was... a hole in the ground. I could see right away what had happened. It was a terrible sight."

"Yes. We saw it ourselves. And then you took your watch and smashed it to pieces?"

"Yes. I threw it against a rock several times."

"Why?"

"So people would find it and see that it was mine. And then think that I was the one who—"

"Who had blown yourself up? That was a little naive after your studies on the effects of explosives. There wouldn't have been anything left of a watch that had been in Mogensen's vest pocket."

"No, it wasn't well thought out."

"But otherwise things seem quite well thought out. When did you get the idea of changing roles with Mogensen?"

"It was out on the Common. When I saw what had happened. When I saw how completely Mogensen had been obliterated. Then I thought that it could — could just as easily have been me."

"You didn't think about disappearing until you were out on the Common?"

"That's right. That's when I made the actual decision. I had sort of . . . sort of fantasized a little about it before."

"When did you start to 'fantasize' about it?"

"It was when I won the money."

"And then a good opportunity came along?"

"Yes, then an 'opportunity' came along."

"And then you wrote your 'suicide note'?"

"Yes."

"Why did you write it to the office and not to your wife?"

"I didn't want her to have such a sudden shock. And of course I knew how the mail was handled at the office. A certain amount of time would elapse —"

"So you wanted to gain some time! Shouldn't we leave your considerate feelings for your unfortunate wife out of your story? We don't have a very high opinion of your sense of consideration! But now tell us, why did you want to *disappear*?"

Yes. Why? That's what Head Clerk Amsted can't answer. He had fantasized for a long time. He had dreamed and romanticized about a life of freedom. About an existence in which he had control over himself. A quiet life in the country. In the region he had known as a child, which represented a vacation paradise to him.

He had sat in the easy chair in his study and dreamed himself away from Herluf Trollesgade and the War Ministry and his superiors at home and at the office. Then came the money. And Mogensen's suicide. The suicide that completely obliterated Mogensen, so it could just as easily have been Teodor Amsted who had been obliterated. On top of everything else, Mogensen was wearing Amsted's discarded suit. Circumstances had converged. It had suddenly become possible to realize his dream.

Why? It wasn't easy to explain to a policeman. He had acted so impetuously. Then it was too late to undo things. He had given in to the desire to play hooky. And he hadn't thought about the consequences.

They ask their questions over and over. His answers don't satisfy the police. They don't understand the eternal schoolboy of 46 who plays hooky and goes out in search of adventure.

"And so you called yourself *Herbert Johnson*. That wasn't a name you chose at random. There was a real Herbert Johnson in the United States. He was also one of your classmates—his name was Herbert Jensen then. It was very clever to take a Danish-American's name. It was a good way to get into the system as someone who was returning from abroad. And your census form and your income tax return have been filled out under a false name.

"It looks rather well thought out and premeditated, Teodor Amsted! You even made sure to acquire some dollar bills so it would really look convincing. Oh yes, we've talked with the bank. And we've corresponded with Herbert Johnson!"

The police know quite a bit, all right.

"And then you had your mustache shaved off." The police know about that too. "It was to make you unrecognizable, wasn't it? But it wasn't very smart to have it done in a small town. And then you bought yourself glasses with ordinary window glass in them. And you did that in the same small town. And you read in the county newspaper about vacant apartments in the country. And you responded to Jens Jensen's advertisement."

The police know most of it. But they aren't satisfied at Police Headquarters. They keep on asking questions.

Then Teodor Amsted, LL.B., is assigned a defense attorney.

For the present, charges of insurance fraud and income tax evasion have been lodged against him.

But perhaps others will be added.

[46]

No FURTHER CHARGES are filed against him.

No indictments are brought for other matters.

And his defense attorney tells him that he's been rather lucky.

He has avoided a lot of trouble and additional scandal and public attention. The fact is, the police had a theory; they had clung to it stubbornly and tenaciously, but they had to give it up.

They thought that he had *murdered* Mikael Mogensen.

Murdered Mogensen? But why on earth would he murder Mogensen?

Yes. Why? The police had theorized that perhaps Mogensen had been extorting money from Amsted. They could not understand why the head clerk supported the peculiar man from Rosengade.

And they couldn't discover any motive for Mogensen to commit suicide either.

Poverty? Mogensen was a philosopher and despised the common material goods of life. And besides, Amsted had given him 1000 kroner. Why should he grow tired of life at precisely the moment he received a gift of such a large sum of money?

And then of course there was the fact that it would appear to be so much easier for a government official in the War Ministry to procure explosives than it would for the solitary, impoverished Mogensen.

The police had based their theory on a number of items. But it had been impossible to obtain conclusive evidence. So now the decision has been made not to bring an indictment for murder. The police will have to be content with the circumstances already mentioned.

But that's plenty.

It means the ruin and downfall of Head Clerk Amsted. It means the loss of his position. It means the loss of his pension. It means the loss of his civil rights. It means disgrace and banishment from his circle of friends and acquaintances.

It means economic ruin. His life insurance will have to be paid back with interest. As well as the pension which had been paid out to his wife. And there is the fine to the Department of Internal Revenue. And there are damages and legal costs.

And perhaps divorce and alimony will be added. Mrs. Amsted wanted to pay him a visit and talk with him. But that couldn't be done. They were able to negotiate only through their lawyer.

She is shattered and inconsolable. Her husband's return has been a much harder blow for her than his death. And now what? What about financial questions? Everything has changed, of course. Everything that had been attained by good upbringing and teaching and education. The whole basis of their existence. The apartment on Herluf Trollesgade will probably have to be given up. The old furniture will have to be sold.

And Leif—there probably won't be enough money to send him to the university now. What will become of him? How will he get along without going to school and studying until he's 25? Yes, it's primarily for Leif's sake. Is he really not going to become a capable government official and esteemed citizen like his forefathers?

There are a lot of problems and a lot of questions.

There is a grave at Assistens Cemetery. A grave with a gravestone and plantings and gravel and everything. It has been purchased for a period of 40 years. Maintenance for another man's grave has been bought and paid for. What's going to happen now?

Teodor Amsted doesn't know. He cannot make any dispositions concerning his own grave. He is imprisoned and without any responsibility. He has been freed from many things.

There will probably have to be some discussion with Mikael Mogensen's family, if he has any. But Teodor Amsted cannot negotiate. It's a good thing to be under arrest in these circumstances.

Teodor Amsted does not apply for release on bail when the preliminary investigation has been concluded. He does not insist on being set at liberty before his case goes to trial. And he does not request permission to talk with his wife.

There are a lot of problems. A lot of misfortunes have befallen the Amsted family.

Still, the arrested head clerk has been lucky. One thing he *has* escaped. The charge of murder will not be lodged.

There is only fraud against the insurance company and forgery of documents and tax evasion left.

It adds up to eight months in prison.

Teodor Amsted does not wish to appeal.

[47]

ORDER HAS RETURNED to Teodor Amsted's life.

His day is divided up. He has something to do. Everything makes sense.

His work consists of pasting paper bags together. This doesn't demand any outstanding talent or reflection. But it does demand punctiliousness and order. And that's something Teodor Amsted has. He has been learning it from the time he was seven years old.

He cuts the edges and folds them and smears on the adhesive with the greatest precision, making certain not to waste any glue. It doesn't go fast. But it's done correctly. And he receives praise for his nice work.

It's monotonous, but no more monotonous or tedious than his work in Section 14 of the War Ministry. It is exactly on a par with what he is used to. He needs precisely those qualities that have been instilled in him.

That's the way it is with everything in here.

The meals are served at regular intervals, the same wholesome, middle-class diet that he has always had and has learned to like. The same fish balls and celery sauce his mother and his wife made and which, over the course of 40 years, he has trained himself to eat up. The same rice pudding and the same chopped meat dishes that he has eaten every single day of his life. And it is served right on time just like at home.

There aren't any problems with firewood or laundry or clean socks here.

The central heating system functions impeccably. There are people who see to it that the temperature is what it's supposed to be. He doesn't have to worry about that sort of thing.

And every week they lay clean wool socks out for him. Just the way his mother and wife did. "There you are. Here's a shirt! Put it on, please! And here's a clean handkerchief!"

The homeless man has again come into ordered circumstances. Tranquility has returned to his life, as well as profound and intense well-being.

There's no fear of nature or shrieking owls or ominous nighttime noises here. He doesn't need to be afraid of break-ins or attacks. The door is properly locked. Whether it's locked from the outside or the inside is really quite immaterial.

Every day he gets a reasonable amount of exercise and fresh

air. The walk in the prison yard takes place at a set time. Just like his stroll along Langelinie every Sunday morning. Or his walk to and from the office. There are paving stones in the prison yard. And he makes sure not to step on the cracks between the stones.

In the evening he can read books from the prison library. They're the same respectable, harmless books that his wife always borrowed from the lending library.

Everything is like it was before.

But actually it's better than it was before. Before, he was just lonely. But he was never alone. He always had to answer questions and be accountable for things. He had to scold Leif and make peace. He had to struggle with the boy's German compositions and math assignments. He had to think about the family's finances. He had to be talkative and entertaining at parties which his position demanded that he host at appropriate intervals. He had to dress up in a tuxedo when they went to dinner at the homes of people who also visited them. He had to put up with insults and humiliations from his Section Chief.

But there are none of these afflictions here. Everything for which he has striven his entire life has been fulfilled. Here there is security and order and cleanliness and regularity and peace of mind. It is as if he has attained a goal. He has attained what he educated himself for during many years of school. Through grade school and high school and the university and tutoring and innumerable examinations.

He sleeps well at night. His appetite is good. His stomach is fine. But if he should happen to get sick, the prison doctor will come right away. He is safe and secure in every respect.

He has attained everything that was held up to him as the best in life. He has attained the highest ideal of bourgeois society.

[48]

He would be completely happy if it weren't for the fact that he knew someday things were going to be different.

This blissful condition is not a permanent one. He will be permitted to spend only a limited time under these circumstances, which correspond so precisely to what he has prepared himself for. Only for a few months will he be able to enjoy the order and regularity and predictability and security for which his family and thousands of middle-class families have striven for generations.

One day he will be released.

One day he will be pushed out into a harsh and uncertain world. A world he doesn't understand and has never learned to understand.

He counts the days and the weeks. When half his time has run out, the second half passes with tremendous speed. There are still months to go. But the months will pass. No power on earth can hold them back.

Teodor Amsted is not equipped to live in the world. The preconditions for his existence no longer apply. His career has been cut short. And he is incapable of living in any manner but the one he was brought up and educated and preordained for.

His path has taken him from the gray school to the red building. He has adapted to a small, limited portion of human existence. And if he steps off his path, he is lost.

There is only one thing to do. He can do something that will bring him back to the prison which fulfills so exactly his demands on life.

He can commit a crime. A true crime. A great and dreadful deed that will be rewarded with life imprisonment.

He does not have a criminal temperament. He is no rebel or enemy of society. He has been a law-abiding citizen and a lover of order. But only a criminal act can bring him in under the ordered conditions that are a prerequisite for him to live.

He has come up with a plan. He has reached a great and terrible decision.

He sits smiling while he works. He pastes his bags carefully and neatly. But he's thinking about his future.

Someday he will be released. But he will make sure that he's able to come back.

Teodor Amsted is smiling. Because nobody in the prison knows that this compliant, diligent, orderly man has decided to become a murderer.

He is smiling. Because he has suddenly become the world's mightiest man. He can point to a person and say: "You are going to die." He can carry out his judgment on anybody he wants. No one can do a thing to him for it. Even if he murders a hundred people, nothing more can happen to him than having his wish fulfilled. The only thing that can happen to him is that he will be allowed to live his entire life in that ideal state which is the goal of all middle-class education and schooling and ambition.

So who is he going to murder? Who is the world's mightiest man going to point to? Is there anyone he hates so passionately that he wants to pass his death sentence?

Teodor Amsted has no enemies. He doesn't hate anyone. Except maybe for...

Yes. He has made his choice. The only person he can think of killing is his former boss. Section Chief Ohmfeldt in Section 14 of the War Ministry is the man he will point to.

Teodor Amsted is not vindictive. He is not bitter and full of hate. He doesn't remember an insult through all eternity. He doesn't store up every affront and injury. But now he tries to recall all the humiliations he has been subjected to. He forces himself to remember what has happened to him.

He remembers the insulting way the Section Chief would look at him and declare that it was deplorable that a government official in the War Ministry was capable of permitting an obvious spelling error in an official document to get by him. It should be assumed, after all, that one of the prerequisites for a person employed in the Ministry would be the possession of sufficient academic background, enabling him, at the least, to be conversant with the country's authorized orthographic conventions. The Section Chief had taken out his ill humor on him so the entire staff could hear. And his subordinates had snickered.

There had been many insults of this kind. There was the time, when he was still a deputy clerk, that he had inadvertently happened to read the noon newspaper before the man whose father had been the Secretary to the Royal Privy Council. And he remembers the Section Chief's reprimand on that occasion. And there was the dinner party at the Section Chief's home where he was assigned a place at the table which was beneath the social rank to which he belonged.

There were the two coat hooks — the Section Chief took possession of both of them, using one for his overcoat and the other for his umbrella, whereas Head Clerk Amsted's overcoat was relegated to a demeaning nail.

There were thousands of little pinpricks during his daily routine at the office. It was essential to remember them now that the Section Chief had to die.

He sits smiling over his paper bags and his glue.

This is no ordinary prisoner. This is a man who has made a great and fateful decision. This is the world's mightiest man who sits pasting bags and folding their edges and being praised by the supervisors.

This is a man who has power over life and death.

[49]

Everything will reach an end.

It might take an infinitely long time. But someday it will reach an end. Every road eventually reaches its end, no matter how long it might be.

When you're young, you think you're never going to die. But someday the moment will arrive anyway. This is unerringly certain. When you're going to school, you think you'll never be finished. But one day you're so changed and so molded and so harmless that you can be let out. When you've been sentenced to a prison term, the time seems eternally, infinitely long. But one day your sentence will be served. One day you will again be permitted to go out into the world. Eventually that day will be reached too. Everything reaches an end.

Time passes.

It is time that determines your professional advancement. The gentleman who feeds the pigeons at the red building during his lunch break will reach retirement age someday. And then someone else can move up to his rank.

Deputy clerks become head clerks with the passage of time. And head clerks become divisional managers and section chiefs as time passes. And a section chief can even become a department head after a long, long time has passed.

Eight months in prison is a long time. It's almost a year. It's many, many weeks and days and mornings.

But eight months will pass too. You can look forward to the day when you will be released. Or you can be afraid of it. But the day will eventually arrive.

And the day for former Head Clerk Amsted's release also arrives. His personal clothing has been returned to him. He has received a small sum of money which he earned pasting paper bags. He has received words of praise from the prison warden for his good behavior.

Early one morning the prison guard opens the large portal of Vestre Prison. And Teodor Amsted can walk down Vigerslev Allé a free man.

He could have been picked up by his wife. But he didn't want that. He could have been visited by her in prison, but he declined.

He bears no malice toward her. But what would they talk about?

He's only going to be in the outside world a short time. He only needs to accomplish one deed. Then he will return to a stable, secure, and lasting environment.

It's cold in the outside world. The wind is blowing down Vigerslev Allé. Teodor Amsted is freezing in his heavy winter coat. No one can tell that this is the world's mightiest man, who has power over life and death.

He has a plan to carry out. It has been thought out in every detail. First he has to buy something in a hardware store. But the stores aren't open yet. He will have to wait a few hours before he can begin his plan.

Two hours is a long time to walk the streets. But two hours will eventually reach an end too. He walks through the streets and waits. He's freezing and he isn't used to walking.

A fragrance drifts out onto the street from a coffee bar. He stops and inhales the sweet aroma.

Somewhat hesitantly he walks inside. He has never been in a place like this before. When he was a head clerk, he would never have dared drink a cup of coffee at a street vendor's cart or in a cheap bar.

Nervously and anxiously he orders coffee and rolls. He cautiously carries the tray with the large steaming cup on it over to a vacant seat.

He takes a cautious sip from his cup. This is probably dangerous, isn't it? Isn't this cup dirty and infected? He will soon be sentenced to life imprisonment. And he's afraid of infection and disease.

His mother would be appalled if she saw him drinking coffee here. And his wife would be shocked. This is something risky and unheard of that he's doing. But the coffee is hot and good and bracing.

Some workmen are sitting in the coffee bar. Some of them are on their way home from night jobs and have dirt and grease on their clothes. Others are just beginning and are drinking their morning coffee here.

The former head clerk looks at them timidly out of the corner of his eye. He instinctively brushes a few flakes of dust from his overcoat.

He has always been slightly afraid of people dressed in work clothes. This is a world he doesn't know. These are people he should keep his distance from. "Don't get too close!" they told him when he was a child.

People dressed in work clothes. They're associated with coarseness and brutality and crude language and the danger of being assaulted.

He has seen craftsmen making repairs in his apartment on Herluf Trollesgade. But he has never spoken with a workman. He was a schoolboy and a university student and a government official, and he only knows other schoolboys and univerity students and government officials. The people he has seen on the street dressed in work clothes are something that belongs to another world.

But no one assaults him as he drinks his coffee.

The workmen are talking and smoking and reading the morning paper. They seem to feel right at home. Maybe they feel as much at home as the people in Section 14 of the War Ministry as they read the noon newspaper in the proper order of rank or drink their afternoon cup of tea from disinfected cups with their little fingers extended.

They have dirt on their work clothes. But they don't do any harm to the newly released head clerk.

Now the stores are beginning to open.

He stands in front of the window of a hardware store looking at the hammers and axes that are hanging neatly arranged in long rows. Then he goes into the store.

"Yes indeed, sir. A *hammer*. Does it have to be any particular type?"

"A good, sturdy hammer."

"Yes indeed. Here's a so-called fitter's hammer. It's a marvelous hammer, sir. It packs a nice wallop. It's very nicely balanced... And then there's this one. If you'd rather have one that can also be used to pull out nails.... It might be a little more practical."

"No, that isn't necessary. It doesn't need to pull out nails... What does this one cost?"

"One-fifty, sir. It's a good hammer. You'll get a lot of use out of it. We sell a lot of those, sir."

"And that one?"

"It only costs 1.25. But it's also an excellent hammer... Then there's this one for 1.75. It's, well, a little sturdier."

Teodor Amsted tries out the various hammers. He weighs them in his hand. He tests their impact. There's one that's pointed on one end and round on the other. It might be particularly well suited.

"What does that one cost?"

"That's a special hammer. It's a little more expensive. It costs 3.75. But it *is* an extra fine hammer. It packs a real wallop. Here, try it yourself."

Teodor Amsted lifts and weighs and tests it. He levels a firm and steady gaze at the sales clerk's forehead. He calculates the distance and hefts the hammer. The sales clerk gets a very funny feeling.

"He looked at me with murder in his eye," he later tells the police.

"This will do just fine." But perhaps he ought to take one of those cheap ones instead? He is an economical man. He thinks it over a little. But then he takes the expensive one after all, the one that's pointed on one end and round on the other. No expense should be spared on an occasion like this. And what does money mean to him now?

"Thank you. I'll take the one for 3.75 ... No. You don't have to wrap it up. I'll take it as it is. I can carry it in my inside coat pocket."

It's still early in the day. He can't visit people now.

The Section Chief won't be starting for home until 5 o'clock. Then he'll have to eat dinner. He's a bachelor. Maybe he'll eat out. And this last meal shall be granted to him.

He can't visit him until around 7:30.

That's a long time to wait. That's a lot of hours to wander through the streets. But eventually it will be 7:30. Everything will reach an end.

[50]

SECTION CHIEF OHMFELDT is at home alone. He's sitting warm and cozy sorting through his collection of military memorabilia.

He's sitting humming and softly singing old battle songs.

"And their former chief, Olaf Rye, they saw — they saw — they saw — anew."

He is full of contentment and satisfaction. He fears no evil. He doesn't know that something is threatening him. He is without anxiety. And when the doorbell rings, he is not frightened. He doesn't know that standing outside is a man with a heavy hammer in his inside coat pocket. He doesn't know that the Angel of Death is ringing his front doorbell.

He is sitting puttering with his collection of uniform buttons. They are neatly arranged in small boxes. Some of them are sewn onto shields of red velvet. Ever since he was a child playing with marbles, he has been collecting uniform buttons. He has buttons from every branch of the armed forces, from every country, and from every historic period.

He has genuine silver buttons from old-time officers' coats. He has bone buttons from the Royal Guards' leggings from the 18th century. He has brass buttons from the Civil Guard of Copenhagen. He has tin buttons from the American Civil War. He has buttons made from stags' antlers from an old Austrian Alpine Regiment. He has buttons from firemen and mailmen and policemen and night watchmen and meter readers and pallbearers and Tivoli guardsmen.

He has epaulettes and badges and stripes and emblems and bands and shoulder straps and tassels and galloons. He has several hundred trouser stripes from artillerymen and dragoons from all over the world. He has hat guards from the venerable militia of Møn and aiguillettes from the Balkans and belts from Morocco and saber sashes from Montenegro.

And on his walls hang sabers and rapiers and swords and cutlasses and daggers and poniards and bayonets. Small artillery shells stand on his desk acting as paperweights.

There are enough weapons to meet any foe. But Section Chief Ohmfeldt has no enemies. He isn't prepared for an attack. He fears nothing.

He hums as he walks out to open the door when the bell rings. He doesn't know that the world's mightiest man is ringing his front doorbell.

Former Head Clerk Amsted is very pale. He is pale after his eight-month prison term. And he is pale at the thought of the deed that has to be carried out.

The Section Chief stands in the doorway looking at him. He looks at him with great astonishment.

"I must say that this amazes me—I hadn't expected this. I would have thought that you would have been in possession of so much... so much *tact* that you would have spared me your visit. This is very embarrassing. *Very* embarrassing."

Footsteps are heard farther down the stairs.

"You'd better come inside. I wouldn't like it if anyone saw you here. That would be very embarrassing. Extremely embarrassing... You really *must* understand that I am in no position to welcome you to my home after what has happened."

He walks in through the hallway. And Teodor Amsted follows close behind. He has taken his hat off and he is holding one hand inside his overcoat.

The Section Chief doesn't speak. He doesn't offer his former head clerk a chair. He sits down at his desk and turns his back to his visitor.

He opens one of the compartments in the desk and hunts for something. Teodor Amsted is standing directly behind his chair. And he is looking at the back of the Section Chief's head. He doesn't see anything else in the room. All the buttons on the large table. The artillery shells on the desk. He doesn't see any of this. He merely stares at the Section Chief's head.

There's only a little hair on it. The top of his head is bald and shiny. There's sort of a little dent in the middle of it. And there are small, delicate blue veins beneath the skin.

He has a firm grip on the hammer and stares at the bald head. He measures the distance and makes his calculations. Should he strike right in the middle where the dent is? Or perhaps a little to the side would be better? At the temple? Should he use the round end of the hammer? Or should he plant the pointed end in the top of the Section Chief's head? He measures and deliberates. Now's the time — now — now ... His sweaty fingers have a firm grip on the handle of the heavy hammer.

It takes the Section Chief a while to find what he's looking for. He doesn't turn around a single time. He can feel the former head clerk standing close behind him. He can hear him breathing.

He hunts in his desk. He pulls out a clean envelope. And he takes a 10-kroner bill from another drawer.

Teodor Amsted sees it all. But he is also looking at the little dent in the top of the Section Chief's head. He sees the small blue veins too.

Slowly and carefully the Section Chief puts the 10-kroner bill into the envelope. He moistens his finger and seals up the envelope. Then he turns around very slowly in his chair.

Amsted is holding his hat in his left hand. He keeps his right hand inside his overcoat.

"Here ... here is a little ... envelope. Please. And then I must urgently request you not to pay me any more visits. I will not be in a position to help you any further. Here!"

He holds out the envelope. And Amsted lets go of the hammer in his inside pocket and accepts the envelope with his sweaty hand.

"Thank you," he mumbles. "Thank you — that was very ..."

The Section Chief gives him a deprecatory wave of the hand. "You cannot expect to receive anything else. And I hope you understand that in the future you must stay away from here."

Amsted has stuffed the envelope into his pocket and hesitantly reaches out his hand to thank him. But the Section Chief doesn't see it.

"You'll have to leave now! But wait — let me go first. I just want to make certain that there's no one on the stairs."

And again Teodor Amsted follows his former boss down the long hallway. He has an envelope in his pocket. And a heavy hammer.

"There's no one on the stairs. I must ask you to hurry. I don't want you to be seen by anyone!... No—don't thank me. Just hurry.... And then never again! Do you hear! I demand that you never show your face here again!"

The front door slams shut.

Former Head Clerk Amsted walks slowly down the stairs.

[51]

Teodor Amsted is lying in an odd iron bed, unable to sleep.

The bed has large brass knobs on it. And the mattress moans and groans every time he turns over.

The New Testament is lying on a white-painted nightstand beside the bed. There are some small religious tracts lying on it too, and on the wall there are adages hanging in fretwork frames.

This is a Temperance Hotel. In the area near Copenhagen's main railroad station. You can hear the trains down in the railroad yard. And you can hear the streetcars on Bernstorffsgade, and the automobiles.

The streetlights cast curious beams of light onto the ceiling through the patterns of the curtains, forming the most peculiar figures. A drunk on the street below is shouting loudly. And some girls are laughing. Teodor Amsted thinks of Hageholm's boisterous voice. And he thinks about Jens Jensen's Karen who never laughed. And about a girl named Alice, who had too much to drink once and wasn't allowed to call home to the historic inn.

He thinks about many things. It's chaotic and confusing. He

groans beneath the Temperance Hotel's cotton blankets. He is feverish like the time he was lying underneath Jens Jensen's musty comforter. He thinks and thinks.

He wanted to commit a murder. For one day he was the world's mightiest man, who could kill whoever he wanted to. All he needed to do was point to a person and say: He shall die! No one could do anything to him for it.

He has a hammer in his coat pocket. And a 10-kroner bill in his jacket pocket. He accepted the bill and said thank you and left. And he left the hammer in his inside pocket, new and unused. It cost 3.75. It was a special hammer with a fabulous wallop.

He sees the top of the Section Chief's bald head with the little dent in the middle. That was where the hammer was supposed to be planted. Nothing stood in his way. The opportunity couldn't have been better. There was plenty of time.

But Teodor Amsted is incapable of killing anybody.

He has committed insurance fraud and forgery. He has been punished and has forfeited his civil rights. He has been shut out. He has nothing to lose. He has been raised above everything. But he cannot murder anyone.

And yet, they suspected him of murder once. They thought that he had blown up poor Mikael Mogensen with dynamite.

Yes. That's what they thought about him. And maybe they still do.

Perhaps this is where his salvation lies.

Teodor Amsted sits up in bed. He grows hot with excitement. The blood rushes to his head.

Here is his salvation! Here is his *murder*!

The main thing now is to think clearly. Easy there! Easy! Important matters have to be considered now!

He thinks and thinks. And he laughs triumphantly. He is not a man who could murder somebody. But what difference does that make, as long as people believe he is?

He has an entire night to think. And an entire day.

But the main thing is to be careful. Ah—the main thing is to be cautious and cunning.

It has to be gone over and rehearsed very carefully. But he has time. There are many difficulties to be negotiated. It isn't easy to be convicted for a crime you haven't committed.

You have to be on your toes. You have to take everything into consideration. Nothing must be left out of your calculations. Everything has to add up. It is more difficult to obtain evidence for a contrived charge than it is to obtain a false alibi.

Teodor Amsted has to summon up all his shrewdness. All the imagination that might possibly be left over after his many years of schooling has to be brought to bear. And all the meticulousness and conscientiousness he has learned must be exploited. He will have to use all his legal studies and his knowledge of the law and jurisprudence.

It will be a big help to him that the police already had their suspicions about him. It will make his job easier. Still, the main thing is to keep a cool head. The main thing is to be ready for any question. This will be his last great examination. If he can pass it, he is saved.

What can his motive have been for murdering Mogensen? Here, of course, the police have already found a motive that he can use. Mogensen was a blackmailer, naturally. Honest Mikael Mogensen's posthumous reputation will have to be sacrificed. He knew something about Amsted. It might have been something about an affair with a kiosk lady, for instance—an affair that Mrs. Amsted wasn't supposed to know anything about.

He had already paid Mogensen small sums of money. And when he won the lottery, he gave him a thousand kroner. But Mogensen was insatiable. He was a vulture, a shark. And he wrote to the Ministry. He sent the letter via messenger and threatened him with a scandal. And then they were supposed to meet out on the Common.

Wasn't that an unlikely place? Yes, it was. But Mogensen was an eccentric, half-mad person. And it had to be a meeting that had been set for some time. The letter was only the last reminder from Mogensen.

It will not be easy to carry out. There will be technical fine points he will have to master. It's fortunate that he was studying explosives in connection with a report on a project for the War Ministry.

Where did he get the dynamite? And how did he manage to get it planted on Mogensen? He must have made ingenious and extensive preparations. He must have been fiendishly clever. He might perhaps have given Mogensen a new overcoat as a gift. An overcoat with dynamite and diabolical devices in all the pockets. He might perhaps have treated a cigar with explosives? — Watch it now! Don't mix too many things together! Be careful!

Cleverly and systematically Teodor Amsted joins link upon link. He stretches his ingenuity to its limits. He prepares himself for his examination with unprecedented thoroughness.

It's a good thing that he's a government official in the War Ministry. It's a good thing that he was one of the people who inspected the Army's laboratory and powder magazines and ammunition depots. It's a good thing that he was working on calculations about explosives and had technical manuals lying on his desk. And as far as the books about explosives that were found in Mogensen's lodgings are concerned: Amsted lent them to him, naturally, so that people would think that Mogensen had committed suicide. That's how fiendishly clever he was.

It's a good thing that he's used to examinations. And it's a particularly good thing that the police had their suspicions and a theory which they only grudgingly gave up; its confirmation will now be viewed as a vindication. And it's a good thing that he has a heavy hammer in his overcoat. A special hammer that no ordinary person would think of buying. It's a good thing that he can confess that he wanted to murder Section Chief Ohmfeldt too. — So why didn't he do it? . . . What's he supposed to answer to that? Of course, he can answer that the Section Chief's apartment was bristling with weapons. That it was impossible to carry out his plan against a heavily armed man!

So perhaps the visit to the Section Chief's apartment wasn't in vain after all.

Now he has to put his thoughts in order. Now everything has to be prepared.

There is a lot he'll have to go through. There will be an interrogation and the reconstruction of the crime and preliminary investigations and a mental observation and a trial.

It will be the biggest and most dangerous examination of his life. But he will pass it, just like he passed the others.

That evening Teodor Amsted directs his steps to Police Headquarters. He is pale from nervousness. He is reporting for his last, decisive examination.

And during a nighttime interrogation he confesses to a terrible crime.

[52]

MRS. AMSTED IS SAILING across a body of water.

This was prophesied to her. And now it is being fulfilled. Still, it is really rather strange.

She is on her way to Aarhus. She has an older, unmarried brother there that she'll be keeping house for. He is a head teacher at the state school. A scrupulous and conscientious man who for more than 30 years has explained to successive generations the difference between separable and inseparable verbs in German grammar.

He lives in a villa on the outskirts of the city. A somewhat older, gray house with bow windows and a little garden in front with boxwood and roses and gravel in it.

And in his rooms is the old furniture from their childhood home. Mrs. Amsted is looking forward to seeing the furniture again. The old home with all its memories. The little bureau, the two empire mirrors, the old clock, and all the rest.

The home on Herluf Trollesgade has been broken up. The furniture has been sold and dispersed. Mrs. Amsted took along only what was necessary to furnish the room that is to be her own private quarters.

Teodor Amsted's portrait has been removed from its leather frame. But she has the frame with her. Perhaps it can be used for something else someday.

She is wearing black. She is more a widow than ever. She is, so to speak, a double widow. She has lost her husband completely and absolutely. She can't even control his soul. He is being administered by other powers now.

She will try to forget that he was ever alive. She will try to protect Leif from the shame and disgrace that has befallen them. She and Leif will take a different name. They can't have the same name as a murderer and a convict. They will live their quiet life in the unfamiliar city where nobody knows them.

She has settled her accounts with the past. The furniture has been sold. But in Aarhus other furniture awaits her which she can protect and take care of. The old, cherished furniture of her childhood home.

She is sailing across a body of water. But this is no uncertain journey. In a way the Aarhus steamship is bringing her home.

And Leif will have a new home. There wouldn't have been enough money to keep him at the boarding school under the altered circumstances. But now he will be able to get into his uncle's good school. And he will receive all the education and all the examinations that are necessary to mold him into a good citizen.

Mrs. Amsted is thinking of Leif. She is thinking of many things. It really was a good thing that the beautiful, shiny card table with its double leaves wasn't sold as well.

This isn't some unknown and uncertain existence that they are entering into. She knows her brother. She is familiar with his home. And she is familiar with every single piece of furniture in his house. She will know how to safeguard his home and his furniture.

She is sailing across a body of water. Olsen's prophecy has been fulfilled. Perhaps his other prophecy will be fulfilled too. Perhaps she will be happy among her childhood home's old mahogany furniture in the gray villa in Aarhus.

[53]

Silent night, holy night,
All is calm, all is bright.

THE CAROL ASCENDS in the white-painted sanctuary. Christmas Eve in the prison church.

The pastor has spoken about childhood Christmases. About the home. About Father and Mother. It wasn't difficult for him to move his congregation. Prisoners are emotional and cry easily. They are easy to influence. Perhaps that's the reason they're here now, because they were so easy to influence.

With their powerful voices they join in singing the old Christmas carol.

Round yon Virgin, mother and child,
Holy infant so tender and mild

They sit there in their freshly pressed gray uniforms looking up at the altar's gilded cross and the Christmas tree. They are men of all age groups and from all walks of life. There are burglars, pimps, assailants, and robbers. There are also several murderers among them.

One of them was once a head clerk in the War Ministry. He had a good position and a beautiful home. He had bright prospects for a pension. He had every possible reason to be content. Yet there must have been some dissatisfaction smoldering in him. He wanted to find out what it was like to have freedom. A number of circumstances converged, and he got his chance. But he wasn't cut out for freedom. He wasn't brought up for freedom. His life was destined to be under control. Things went all to pieces for him when he got out onto the bounding main.

But he has come home now. He is sitting in the prison church reliving his childhood Christmas. He looks at the Christmas tree and he listens to the carol. He sings along himself:

Radiant beams from Thy holy face

He has reached his goal. Security and peace of mind. Order and predictability. He is here for life. He can look to the future with confidence. He has been pensioned. There is nothing in his existence that does not precisely correspond to the ideals that were held up to him throughout his entire life. Parents and school and the university prepared him for this life. He has reached his goal.

Glories stream from Heaven afar,
Heavenly hosts sing Alleluia

The other prisoners gaze at him. "He's a murderer. He's the one who blew up a guy with dynamite. He looks so helpless. Who would have thought he could do that? But you can't always judge a man by his looks!" They gaze at him in admiration.

Social prestige? Civic standing? Has he forfeited these things? Isn't it a great thing to be a murderer in the little society where he is now? Isn't a murderer better than a burglar or a robber or a common thug? In the world of the prison a murderer belongs to the highest rank. It's almost like being a department head. When the prison newspaper comes out on the first of the month, it goes without saying that Teodor Amsted reads it first.

He has everything now. Even social prestige.

When the worship service is over, the prisoners will have the traditional roast pork and red cabbage and thick brown gravy. They will also have the opportunity to smoke a couple of cheroots. They can sit and lose themselves in their memories—childhood—their parents...

Then the holidays arrive. And when they're over, life continues on its quiet way. There is work to be done and things for them to do. There are several million paper bags that have to be pasted. And precision and conscientiousness are praised.

Not all the prisoners are as content as Teodor Amsted. They are restless people. They haven't had his good upbringing. They haven't been prepared for this life over the course of many, many years. They haven't had the advantage of his schooling. They had too much imagination. They are nonconformists and misfits.

But for Teodor Amsted the meaning of life has been fulfilled. His education is finally complete. He has achieved what he has striven for. He has no further wishes.

Sleep in heavenly peace...

[ABOUT THE AUTHOR]

HANS SCHERFIG wrote *The Missing Bureaucrat* while living with his wife and infant son in a single cramped room rented from a forester in Tibirke, on the northwest coast of Sjælland. This was his second novel, following the success of *The Dead Man* in 1937.

Scherfig was a painter long before he became a writer; the illustration on the front cover is his original artwork for the first edition of *The Missing Bureaucrat* (Den forsvundne fuldmægtig) in 1938. Although this novel was written two years before *Stolen Spring*, it is chronologically a sequel. Scherfig, who liked to use some of the same characters in successive novels, depicted Amsted and Mogensen's school days in *Stolen Spring*, and Mrs. Sylvia Drusse appeared first in *The Dead Man*, as well as in later novels.

Scherfig was also a brilliant amateur zoologist. One lifelong project was to write a scholarly work on the dragonflies of Denmark, a subject in which his expertise exceeded that of the professors, but it was never finished. The photo on the back cover captures him on one of his expeditions to a local pond.

For a more complete biographical sketch, see the Afterword in *Stolen Spring*.

[SELECTED BIBLIOGRAPHY]

Den døde Mand. 1937 (*The Dead Man,* Fjord Press, 1988)
Den forsvundne Fuldmægtig. 1938 (*The Missing Bureaucrat,* Fjord Press, 1988)
Det forsømte Foraar. 1940 (*Stolen Spring,* Fjord Press, 1986)
Idealister. Swedish edition 1944; first Danish printing 1945 (*Idealists,* Fjord Press, 1989)
Skorpionen. 1953 ("The Scorpion")
Krigs-ABC. 1961 ("The ABCs of War")
Frydenholm. 1962 (*Frydenholm,* Fjord Press, 1990)
Den fortabte abe. 1964 (*The Lost Monkey,* Fjord Press, 1989)
Den fattige mands bil. 1971 ("The Poor Man's Car")
Butleren og andre historier. 1973 ("The Butler and Other Stories")
Holberg og andre forfattere. 1973 ("Holberg and Other Authors")
Det borgerlige samfund og dets institutioner. 1974 ("Middle-Class Society and Its Institutions")
Marxisme, rationalisme, humanisme. 1974 ("Marxism, Rationalism, Humanism")

[GLOSSARY OF PROPER NAMES]

Aarhus. Denmark's second-largest city, on the mainland of east-central Jutland.

Amager Common. An extensive open area on the small island of Amager on the east side of Copenhagen harbor. The Danish military once used part of the Common for artillery practice. Signs still warn of buried explosives and urge pedestrians to keep on the paths.

Assistens Cemetery. Close to the center of Copenhagen, in the Nørrebro district. This cemetery is the final resting place of many prominent Danes: Søren Kierkegaard, Hans Christian Andersen, Henrik Pontoppidan — and Hans Scherfig himself.

Bornholm. Scenic Danish island in the Baltic Sea south of Sweden.

Christiansborg Palace. The site of the Danish Parliament.

Dybbøl. A town in southern Jutland which was the scene of a decisive victory by Danish forces over Prussia in 1848 and of a crushing defeat of the Danes by Prussian and Austrian troops in 1864.

Frederik VII (1808–1863). Danish king during whose reign the transition to constitutional government took place.

Frederiksberg. An autonomous borough of Copenhagen directly west of the center and completely surrounded by the city.

Frue Plads. Familiar to readers of *Stolen Spring* as the location of the "gray school," this square is still home to Vor Frue Kirke (Church of Our Lady) and the older section of the University of Copenhagen.

Fyn. The second-largest Danish island, lying between Sjælland and the mainland of Jutland.

Garnison Church. The church nearest to the Amsted apartment on Herluf Trollesgade, not far from the Royal Palace.

Grejsdalen. A scenic valley northwest of Vejle in eastern Jutland.

Grundtvig, N. F. S. (1783–1872). Danish poet, historian, translator, clergyman, and educator. Founder of the Danish Folk High School movement.

Gurre. A village in North Sjælland near Helsingør.

Himmelbjerget. Near the central Jutland city of Silkeborg, this hill ("Heaven Mountain") is one of the highest points in Denmark, at 147 meters above sea level.

Hveger, Ragnhild (b. 1920). Record-breaking Danish swimmer, she won a silver medal in the 1936 Olympics.

Kongens Have. The King's Garden, laid out by Christian IV around Rosenborg Castle in central Copenhagen.

Kongens Nytorv. The King's New Market, the largest square in Copenhagen, is surrounded by venerable landmarks: The Royal Theater, Hotel d'Angleterre, Magasin du Nord, and Nyhavn.

Kullen. A high promontory on the Swedish coast north of Hälsingborg, a favorite tourist attraction.

Leif the Lucky. Leif Eriksson (ca. 970–ca. 1021), Icelandic seafarer who is said to have landed in North America around 1000 A.D.

Lodge, Sir Oliver (1851–1940). British scientist and prolific author of several hundred works on subjects as diverse as physics, psychology, philosophy, religion, education, and spiritism. The book referred to by Sylvia Drusse is doubtless *Raymond, or Life and Death* (1916), in which Lodge described his attempts to communicate with his son who was killed in World War I.

Metropolitan School. Prestigious Copenhagen school founded in 1209. Hans Scherfig attended it and described its flaws in *Stolen Spring*.

Niels Juel (1629–1697). A famous Danish admiral remembered for his victories over the Swedish navy. His statue surveys a square close to Kongens Nytorv.

Oehlenschlæger, Adam (1779–1850). Danish poet and dramatist of the Romantic period.

Queen Louise's Bridge. Crossing the old city moat, it links Nørrebrogade to Frederiksborggade.

Rocambole. Hero of the adventure novels by the French author Pierre-Alexis Vicomte de Ponson du Terrail (1829–1871).

Rosengade. A one-block street not far from Kongens Have. The buildings on this street have been considerably renovated since Hans Scherfig and Mikael Mogensen lived in them.

Rye, Olaf (1791–1849). Norwegian-born military officer best known for his valor in the Dano-Prussian War in 1849.

Sandet. An area in North Sjælland which lies south of Tisvilde Woods on the lake called Arresø.

Slotsholm. A small island in central Copenhagen containing Christiansborg, the Royal Library, and many of the ministry buildings.

Vestre Prison. A formidable-looking prison in Valby, not far from Carlsberg Brewery in the west end of Copenhagen.

[ABOUT THE TRANSLATOR]

FRANK HUGUS (b. 1941) first heard of Hans Scherfig almost twenty years ago while vacationing with friends in the Tisvilde area of North Sjælland. Captivated by *The Missing Bureaucrat*, he proceeded to read Scherfig's other major novels over the course of the next several months. He has been a devotee of Hans Scherfig's works ever since.

While translating this novel, Mr. Hugus returned to Tisvilde several times, sampling something of the flavor of Teodor Amsted's stay there during both the summer and the winter months. While in Copenhagen, Mr. Hugus also visited the places where Teodor Amsted and Mikael Mogensen were formed and molded and lived their lives of quiet desperation.

A native Pennsylvanian, Mr. Hugus first traveled to Europe in 1957. Since 1970 he has taught Scandinavian languages and literatures at the University of Massachusetts at Amherst. He lives in Amherst with his wife and daughter.